A Seabold Fights

by Frederick Faust, writing as

MAX BRAND

Illustrated by

Ralph Pallen Coleman

ADELAIDE & SHEPPARD

Introduction

BY ANDREW SALMON

ONLY A writer as skilled and capable as Frederick Faust (here writing as Max Brand) could pull off an exciting war novel as seen through the lens of a… fruit company? It's a testament to his narrative prowess that Faust delivers an action-packed read that has sat neglected for more than 80 years.

A Seabold Fights is not your typical war novel by any stretch of the imagination. Originally running as a serial in *Maclean's Magazine* (November 15, 1936–February 15, 1937), Faust begins the tale as a typical fish-out-water, coming of age yarn. We are introduced to Joseph Seabold, part of the family that has built the Seabold Fruit Company into a powerhouse outfit. Thing is, young Seabold doesn't give a damn about fruit nor the company that bears his name. But Ronald Seabold, the head of the company is getting up there in age and the years he spent forging the business empire have taken their toll on the revered man. He's anxious to groom a successor but Joe wants nothing to do with the company.

This apathy spurs the aging cousin to send big, strapping Joe down to the Republic of San Esteban as bad things are brewing. The leader of San Esteban was placed in power by Ronald Seabold which gives us an idea of the influence the company has south of the border. Well, the local politicians aren't too happy with the selection and that's just the beginning of the problems awaiting Joe. With revolution in the air, the local company manager out of his depth, the arch rival Universal Fruit Company desire to supplant the Seabold Fruit Company as top dog in the business, things are bad enough but Joe's inadvertent trampling on the sacred traditions of San Esteban as well as refusing to pay off General Easter, the hornets' nest has been soundly kicked and there'll be hell to pay.

It's revolution! And the Seabold name is firmly attached to the government in power, the head of which promptly demands $400,000 from Seabold to fight the rebels and "ensure" that the company retains the vast tracts of land they leased from the government to grow bananas. The threat is obvious and Joe, now the reluctant head of the company, has a choice to make. This all makes for interesting reading but Faust gives us more angles to consider. Joe Seabold doesn't want anything to with the company, let alone picking a side in a revolution. He's all for pulling up stakes and heading home despite how his fleeing the action might look. And his decision to stay has more to do with personal pride than the desire to protect the company's interests.

What follows is a riveting tale as Joe weaves his way through a country at war. With peril at every turn and enemies plotting against him, he finds unlikely allies in the dark heart of the jungle. Not only does Faust give us sweeping battle scenes but the highlight of the novel is the personal struggles the characters face against their enemies, the environment and the testing of their mettle against these odds. From political scheming to canon blasts, *A Seabold Fights* makes for some fine reading.

The novel also provides something of a prophetic glimpse at the author's future. Faust had a thirst for life that would be difficult if not impossible to top. I'm not referring to endless parties with mass consumption of intoxicants or recklessly throwing himself into never ending tests of his manhood or abilities. But, rather, Faust had an insatiable interest in all aspects of life. Any subject that caught his interest, he had to know everything about it. A lover of conversation and debate, his friendly opponents used to be frustrated no end because Faust always seemed to know everything about everything. This makes sense as the prolific author would require an encyclopedic knowledge if he had a hope of writing tales fast enough to stay ahead of his debts. His natural, personal interests in life aided him in his work.

But what does all this have to with *A Seabold Fights?* As stated above, it's a war novel. And war fascinated Frederick Faust. He believed that fighting in battle was the highest level of human experience one could have as no better understanding of life could be attained unless the threat of losing one's life hung over the experience.

Faust loved to drink in all that life had to offer rather than merely write about it and his burning desire to experience war, first hand, would dog him through life and eventually lead to his premature death.

In 1915, while working as a reporter in Hawaii, Faust dropped everything and hopped a steamer bound for Vancouver, Canada. The US had not entered WWI at this point and Faust set his sights on joining the Canadian Army so he could get into battle. The odds were against him as the 6'3", 210 pound Faust suffered from atrial fibrillation and his weakened heart should have kept him out of the army. Except it didn't. In Vancouver he was accepted into the Canadian Army and his dream (or nightmare) of experiencing war first hand seemed within reach. But things didn't move fast enough for eager Faust and, rather than wait for his unit to be shipped overseas, he deserted and headed to Toronto where he was able to join the 97th Canadian Battalion comprised of Americans considered "not too proud to fight" and dubbed the "American Foreign Legion" due to men who comprised it.

Once again, Faust's plans were thwarted as red tape stalled the unit in Nova Scotia awaiting deployment and his machine gun section seemed destined to miss the war altogether. As a result, he was urged to desert again, which he did, walking from New Brunswick to Maine and eventually New York for one last try.

This time he presented himself to the English consulate to see if they could get him across the ocean. With his German name he was considered a spy and turned away. Landing a job working for the subway at William and Beekman streets, Faust's dreams of staring into what one of his characters would later call "the bright face of danger" were over. For now.

The rest is history. Faust suffered the life of the starving artist at the Bowery YMCA until a friend of his recommended he pay a visit to editor Robert H. Davis of The Frank A. Munsey Company that published *The Argosy* and *All-Story Weekly*. The sale of short stories to *All-Story Weekly* ("Convalescence," March 31, 1917) and the pulp career of Frederick Faust began. A career which allowed him to experience peril through the eyes of hundreds of characters.

But if Faust was anything, he was tenacious and stubborn as a mule. Great traits for building and maintaining a writing career. Not so great however when it comes to the burning desire to put his life at risk. No doubt believing he was living on borrowed time due to his heart condition lent an urgency to all he did and the body of work he left behind is infused with that urgency. Pick up a Faust tale and you'll have a lot of trouble putting it down until you've rushed to the end.

The lust for battle never left Faust. Even after the rise of fascism drove him out of the villa he loved in Florence and into the gaping maw of Hollywood and a job at MGM, the need to gain first-hand knowledge of all life had to offer never left him. The work in Hollywood was boring, his heavy drinking was affecting his home life. Now aged fifty, he felt he'd wasted his life churning out pulp tales he considered drivel. So when WWII exploded in Europe, Faust was not going to miss this second opportunity.

Like any good American of the time, he wanted to help with the war effort, starting with what he knew best, writing. Interviewing returned airmen of the 212th Marine Fighter Squadron at El Toro Air Base near Los Angeles, Faust collected their experiences of fighting the Japanese in the South Pacific. His goal was a book commemorating their sacrifices for the war effort. The book would not be published until 1996, more than 50 years after his death. Fighter Squadron at Guadalcanal was Faust's first, and last, non-fiction book. Not being able to land a publisher while working on the book, one can't help but wonder if this lack of success spurred him on to get even more involved in the war.

It was a topic he refused to let go. Faust tried to launch a plan which would see him dropped into the guerilla forces fighting the Nazis in Yugoslavia. When that fell through, he tried to accompany a convoy of US ships bound for Murmansk in Northern Russia.

Then, finally, he hit pay dirt.

He convinced *Harper's Magazine* to hire him as a war correspondent. In February, 1944 he returned to Italy and joined the 88th Infantry Division of the US Fifth Army station 30 miles north of Naples. His job was to live and travel with the front line troops, get to know them, and experience battle whenever they went into action. The end result would be a book examining real battle experiences and their aftermath.

Despite warnings to the contrary, Faust insisted on going in with the first wave against the Nazi troops in the battle of Santa Maria Infante. On the night of May 11th, on the hill leading up to the occupied territory, Faust was struck in the chest by enemy shrapnel and died on the battlefield. He was two weeks shy of his 52nd birthday.

What is uncanny about these tragic events is their similarity to the climactic battle in *A Seabold Fights,* written eight years earlier. Faust sometimes referred to his writing as "dreaming" and any writer of fiction has at one time or another experienced that trance-like state where the actions of a piece of fiction are so real and so immediate, it feels as if one is taking dictation of the events and not imagining them whole cloth. It's a period of instantaneous creation and what results rarely requires extensive revision. Undoubtedly, an author as prolific as Frederick Faust was particularly adept and slipping into this dreaming trance. As a novelist myself I can state for the record that it makes the work go a whole lot faster—something Faust would definitely appreciate with bill collectors and needy friends and relations breathing down his neck.

In this particular scene in the novel, Faust sends tall, strapping Joe Seabold and his men slogging uphill in the mud and the scene has a visceral quality you see, hear and feel: the explosions of enemy fire, the screams of the men, bullets whizzing by your ears, the ground trembling when artillery fire hits. You feel it, you live it. It is some of Faust's best work.

And one can't help but wonder if the "dreaming" Faust in 1936 was seeing his own demise eight years later as he, himself, the tall, strapping soldier scrambled uphill through minefields and barbed wire only to be struck down and killed by the enemy. As he had never been in battle firsthand when he wrote A Seabold Fights, how was he able to capture the feeling of it in the novel when he would not actually experience what his character endured until years later. Was it mere power of imagination or was something deeper working here? The parallels between fiction and reality are striking and worth considering after you have read the scene. Does the fictional Joe Seabold survive the battle? No spoilers. Read the novel and find out for yourself. You'll be glad you did.

As far as I've been able to determine, A Seabold Fights has never been reprinted nor appeared in book form. So unless you've been collecting Faust's work in its original magazine form, few have had the pleasure of reading this adventure tale since the last installment of the serial saw print in early 1937.

Well, you're in for a treat. A Seabold Fights delivers. The novel is well worth the wait. Enjoy!

A Seabold Fights

IN FORMER days Ronald Seabold kept behind his desk for every interview, but when age came on him suddenly, whitening his hair and his face, he formed the habit of moving over to a pair of leather armchairs near the window for important conferences. Here he found a double advantage, because his caller faced somewhat into the light and could see only in part how time had withered the lips of the master of the Seabold Fruit Company; also, the view from the fortieth story over the lesser skyscrapers down to the bridges which arched the river was sure to lead the mind to a clearer conception of the wealth and spreading power of the Seabold Company. Fortunately, his voice remained quite young, which assisted the illusion of unbroken strength. On this morning he wished that illusion to be more perfect than ever, for he was in the midst of what was perhaps the most important conference of his life—and the doctors had told him that he was about to die.

During the opening moments he had talked casually while he studied young Joseph Seabold, who had the second of those big leather chairs, and he wished that he had begun this close study many years before, the moment it became certain that his youthful cousin was to be the heir to the throne. Joseph was a tall, spare young man, except about the shoulders which had gained weight from tugging at a varsity oar; shoulders which were a trifle bowed by the same tennis which had lightened his feet. This gave Joseph a rather studious air, but the older Seabold knew only too well that he was no student.

Joseph was not a handsome lad. There was plenty of brain space in his skull, but the flesh was laid on a little too sparsely over the bones of his face and, for such a good athlete, his neck seemed a bit scrawny. But you can't tell by his looks which hound will catch the fox. Earnestly, with a slight shudder of weakness and of anxiety in his heart, the old man wished that he knew more about the youngster. He had put off the learning, and now it might be too late.

"Now for a more serious theme, Joe," he said, but paused and made a gesture as though he were waiting for proper words to fall into his hand.

"You mean the way I've been dodging it down at the office?" suggested Joseph. "Getting there late, and pretty shoddy work, and all that?"

This readiness at first pleased the head of the firm because he took it for courage; a moment later he knew that it was indifference. He had to rally himself strongly to keep a full voice in his throat.

"You don't like the business, Joe. You've only been at it a month, and you don't like it. Suppose you tell me what's wrong with it?"

"I can't," said Joe. "It's just—bananas!"

JOE LAUGHED a little. Plainly bananas were of no importance. Ronald Seabold, with half-closed eyes, for the moment was breathing the steam of the jungle again and hearing the machetes go swish through the pulpy softness of the green.

"It's far away. You don't like it for that?" asked Ronald.

"No; it's just bananas. I suppose I sound like a fool."

"You don't; I can understand that. Any other sort of business appeal to you?"

"Well—no."

"If I passed out of the picture tomorrow, you'd have a million or so in the bank. In normal times, you could sell out the business for several more millions. Is that what you'd do?"

"If you want the name of Seabold still on the banana boats, I won't sell out," said Joseph.

"What will you do with the property?"

"I'll let Mr. Kelvin take complete charge. I know you trust him."

"I trust him as an ideal private secretary, a perfect office boy, though he has the title of general manager."

Joseph was silent.

"Is there any one thing that you want to do in the world?" asked Ronald Seabold.

Joseph looked up suddenly. "Yes—I don't know," he said.

"Fly over the South Pole, or shoot lions in Africa?"

"Well—I don't know," said Joseph. He smiled a little. There was a bright vision in his eye. "But if Kelvin couldn't run the company, how could I do it?"

"I don't know how. I only know that you'll have to."

"Have to?" said Joseph quietly.

"Yes. You'll have to."

"There's such a thing as not caring a hoot about money," said Joseph.

The old man nodded, because he liked a man who could strike back.

"Suppose I were out of it; somebody started to take the whole thing away from you; would you fight back or sell out?"

"I'd be a fool to play a game where I don't even know the rules."

"You wouldn't be a fool. You'd be a Seabold. Joseph, I want you to go to New Orleans at once and take a boat for San Esteban."

"It's no good," said Joseph. "Getting on the ground wouldn't inspire me. I want to be straight about it… What you did was great. I admire it a lot. You built the thing up and all that. Well, give it to somebody else. Give it to somebody who loves the business and has the brains for it. I don't want a great pile of money. I have enough of my own. You get hold of a real successor and I'll step out of the picture."

He sat forward, ready to rise and end the interview.

"You're going to run down to San Esteban just to please me," said Seabold. "Will you do that, Joe?"

"To please you? Why, I'll go ten times around the world. Of

Mary said: "He doesn't know anything about anything."

"I think he's a Seabold," said Marigny. "I think we'll have to fight."

course I'll go," said Joseph, drawing a big breath. "When shall I start?"

"Now," said Seabold.

"All right, in a day or two I'll—"

"Go now," said Seabold. "Today, before you change your mind. See what you're giving up, and then throw it away if you want to."

"I'll take the next train," said Joseph. "And how long shall I stay down there?"

"You'll know the right time to leave," said Seabold. "Good-bye, my boy."

AFTERWARD, HE watched the long, light step of Joseph leave the room. Even the clumsy weight of brogans could not keep the aspiration from that stride. The knees of Seabold trembled with weakness as he watched; then he summoned Kelvin.

There had been a time when Henry Lewis Kelvin was as keen a filibuster as ever sailed by night into the damp heat of a tropical harbor, but now he was all gray and sleek, and leaned back as he walked to balance the weight he carried before him.

The breath had gone from Seabold during that last interview. Now he eyed Kelvin until it returned to him, and until Kelvin was as serious as an after-dinner speaker, at least.

"If Marigny and the Universal Fruit people go into San Esteban after us," said Seabold, "who will fight them for us?"

"They can't attack us," said Henry Kelvin. "You have the president of the republic in your pocket."

"When I'm gone, my pocket will be gone with me. I mean, suppose that I were out of the way and the Universal bought up Don Ricardo Rodriguez. Who'd there be to fight for us?"

"Why, there'd be General Easter."

"He needs handling."

"There's Robertson to handle him."

"Robertson is like me—old."

"I could go down there myself," said Kelvin.

"You're soft and fat," answered Seabold. "Unless we have someone down there with authority in his hands and a fighting heart, the Seabold Company will be wiped off the slate. All our work out the window. So I've sent Joseph down there."

"Joseph? But he's only..."

"At least he has a name they know," said Seabold. "And he may grow older. It's hot in San Esteban, Harry, and a man ripens fast. If he can last long enough to learn the rules of the game, he may make a fight of it."

"You talk as though you were going to retire," said Kelvin, smiling.

"It's going to be more complete and sudden than retirement, Harry."

At this Kelvin leaned forward until two deep wrinkles were incised in the well-buttoned sleek of his coat. Seabold, gradually lifting his head, let the light fall across his haggard face. The youthful resonance went out of his voice as he concluded: "I've made my will. The moment I'm gone, you wire to San Esteban that Joseph is my sole heir; that everything is in his hands."

"But Joseph..." cried Kelvin. "He doesn't understand. He has no—"

"It's too late for me to teach him," said Seabold, "and no one else knows how. But if you throw a boy into deep water—that's one way of teaching him how to swim, isn't it?"

WHAT HAD been bland spring in the North was thick, hot summer in New Orleans, when Joseph Seabold stepped off the train at the foot of Canal Street. Algiers lay trembling behind the heat waves on the farther side of the river, and the traffic of the old town roared and paused on his ear with a note dreamier than that of Northern cities, he thought. The taxi brought him to the St. Charles Hotel, where the big, shadowy rooms seemed cooler than they were. A drowsiness came upon him. He felt that already he had passed into a far land; and the melancholy sense of change kept increasing until, a few hours later, he was on the levee beside the ship that was to take him to San Esteban.

The boats of the Universal Fruit Company, he knew, were shining white; but the *Avon* of the Seabold Fruit Company was a dingy old craft that fouled the air and herself with clouds of sooty smoke.

The gangplank was such a meagre affair that it sprang slightly beneath his step. As he reached the end of it, the captain greeted him with good, bluff, seamanly courtesy and then led him forward. The captain had the look of a real sea dog, with a complexion compounded of sun, hard gales and Jamaica rum. His name was Ted Binner. As he went forward, he apologized. The owner's cabin had been taken by General Easter before they had known they were to have the pleasure of Mr. Seabold's company. If Mr. Seabold did not object, they would not move all the heavy luggage of General Easter, but try to please Mr. Seabold with the second best accommodation.

"I've heard of Easter," said Joseph Seabold.

The captain almost stopped to look at him, then went hurrying on, silent; and Seabold knew that he had made a mistake. He was taken to a good suite of cabins, the paint a little smoky and rubbed.

"We'll try to make you comfortable," said Captain Binner. "Mr. Seabold's an uncle or something of yours, isn't he?"

"A sort of cousin," said Joseph.

"Oh, a sort of cousin," nodded the captain. "That box yonder has your kit in it. It came aboard a couple of days ago. Let me know if you need anything. You speak Spanish?"

"Yes."

"That's good," said the captain, and departed.

Seabold studied the kit-box with gloomy interest. If it had been brought on board two days before, he could be sure that Ronald

Seabold had been certain of his power to force him to take the trip. The diplomacies of an old codger like that, he thought, are too transparent; but though they might lead him to the river, they could not make him drink. He already knew the tropics, he felt. The sooty old *Avon* was the sordid foretaste.

Depressed, he went out on deck.

"I thought we were sailing at once?" he said to a sailor.

"Waiting for General Easter, is all," replied the sailor, and laughed.

Now, up the gangplank came a negro boy in a hotel uniform, hanging on to the leashes of a pair of greyhounds, all full of panting, muzzled eagerness. A mulatto woman followed in haste, carrying in both hands a lofty parcel wrapped in tissue paper.

The boy, at the top of the gangplank, gasped: "For General Easter!"

The captain swore. "Here, you! Take these cursed dogs to the top deck!"

A sailor gathered them in; and Captain Binner, scowling, gave a tip to the lad.

"For General Easter, sir," said the mulatto girl.

It was impossible to avoid seeing the contents of the package, for the tissue paper was as transparent as though it had been oiled, and Seabold saw a towering miracle of the hat-maker's art, all aflow and alive with feathers. The captain, taking the parcel, gave to Seabold a glance half-ashamed and half-amused before he carried the hat away in his own hands.

SEABOLD WENT up to the top deck, where the greyhounds were tied to a boat-lashing. The sailor had left the muzzles on, so he freed the heads of the dogs. They began to poke their long, wet noses into his hands like a pair of hungry seals, and he stroked the thin velvet of their necks. His picture of the general was beginning to have a local habitation and a name.

The picture grew more vivid when he heard from below the

voice of Captain Binner saying: "Mister, take three good men and go down to get Jack Easter. Try the Hotel Vincent. Don't stop at asking. Go through the whole place. If you come to a locked door, break it open. Get to work." And presently the first mate, followed by three husky sailors, ran down the gangplank.

Seabold smiled as he watched them. Then he went back to his cabin and opened the heavy kit-box. It contained a small arsenal; a .250-3000 rifle, a super .38 automatic, an automatic twenty-two, and a hunting knife. There were also an electric headlight with ten batteries, a pair of field boots, a wide-brimmed felt hat, riding breeches of a material impenetrable by rain, a coat of the same material of the field-engineer type, a pair of field-glasses, a hypodermic with antitoxin for snakebite, and a neat little surgical kit. He tried the hat and, when he found it a perfect fit, knew that the kit must have been ordered long before and made to his measure. He felt the damp green of the jungle already closing about him.

He rang the bell, and a little, yellow-eyed half-breed answered it.

"Put this stuff away for me, will you?" asked Seabold. "And by the way, tell me something about General Easter. What's he done?"

"General Easter?" echoed the boy, looking around him for means of illustration. Then he laughed. "Why, General Easter—he took San Esteban City with 300 men! General Easter, he..."

His words left him. He made a slow gesture with both hands that included the world. "You don't know about the general?" he asked in complete wonder.

Seabold went back on deck in time to hear an automobile horn that screamed swiftly up the street. The taxi of the first mate was returning, bulging with humanity. Two motorcycles, charging in pursuit, drew up to the car at the curb; two furious policemen dismounted and advanced on the lout that tumbled out of the machine. A tall man, dazzling in white, confronted the officers, leaning on a walking stick that bent a little under his weight.

He had hardly made a gesture before the policemen burst into hearty laughter. Afterward they shook hands with the man in white, and he advanced alone toward the gangplank.

At least he seemed to be alone, for even the first mate fell back a little behind him at the side of a fat little man with a pointed beard and mustaches waxed to long, daggerlike points. The three sailors came shoulder to shoulder at the rear, each carrying a pair of large gilded birdcages.

The captain appeared at this moment on deck.

"I presume that's General Easter?" asked Seabold.

"Easter?" said the captain. "Yes. Yes, that's General Easter."

HE SPOKE in a dream, hardly aware of Seabold, but drinking in with his eyes the approaching figure. General Easter wore a white Panama hat so thin that its brim fluttered in the wind; clothes of almost transparent flannel that must have been specially woven, thought Seabold. There were shoes flawlessly white, and the hand which held the Malacca stick clasped a pair of pale chamois gloves. Yet something was wrong about the lofty figure. It was not in the long, pink face, though the monocle stuck in the right eye was an unusual touch. General Easter was halfway up the gangplank before Seabold noticed that his shirt was fastened at the top by a collar button but the collar itself was missing.

"Ah, Captain Binner," said the general.

"Mighty glad to see you, general," said the captain, he almost bowed over the hand of Easter. "Your cabin is ready."

"The Rhine wine," said General Easter. "You didn't forget it, did you? You wouldn't forget that, captain, would you?"

"It's there," said Binner. "In two buckets of ice."

"You *are* a man to be trusted," said Easter. "Then just give Vincent five hundred for me, will you, and we can sail."

"*Five*—hundred?" said the captain.

"Five hundred even," said the general.

The captain, with startled eyes, drew out a wallet.

"Good-bye, Vincent," said the general. "How old is that blonde girl?"

The fat man clasped his nervous hands together and smiled till the tips of his waxed mustaches were as high as his eyes.

He made a jerking bow as he answered: "Twenty-three, general. Thank you, sir."

"Wonderful!" said General Easter. "At twenty-three she knows Scotch like a sister. A natural philosopher. Give her my compliments and one of those hundreds."

"Sir?" said Vincent, his eyes rolling.

"You French son of a thief," said the general without violence, "I said one of the hundreds."

"Yes, sir," answered Vincent. His body deflated with a sigh; he roused himself to take the money from the captain, who said softly:

"If you put your teeth into the general again, I'll fry you in hell fire, you punk!"

Mr. Vincent fled.

General Easter was saying: "Careful with those cages, my lads… Give them a dollar apiece, Binner, will you, like a good fellow?"

"Yes," groaned Binner. "And—ah—this is Mr. Joseph Seabold, General Easter."

"This is a real pleasure," said the general, giving his hand like a prince. "Making your first trip to San Esteban?"

"First and last," said Seabold.

"Last?" said the general.

He took out his monocle, looked at Seabold, and hastily replaced the glass in his eye. "Ah, too bad, too bad!" said General Easter.

He turned away on legs that were a little unsteady. Seabold saw the captain looking down at the deck, one side of his face working with a strongly repressed smile.

"I wouldn't like to see you without means, left deserted." Seabold pulled out his wallet.

"Gringo dog!" said Rosita.

GENERAL EASTER appeared seldom throughout the voyage. If Seabold asked about the famous man, the captain said the general was indisposed and hastily found another subject for conversation. Everyone acted the same way. It was as though they were drawn into a kinship, a clanhood, by their acquaintance with the

great man and wished at every cost to keep Seabold far from him. For two people in the world they seemed to feel this reverence— the general and Ronald Seabold. A patent difference appeared in their voices when they spoke of "the Admiral—your cousin, Mr. Seabold." If, plainly, there was only one "General" for the men of San Esteban, so there was only one "Admiral," though in all his days Joseph never had heard the nickname applied to his rich cousin. There was even a picture of him on a wall of the captain's dining room, where they gathered three times a day. The painting was in a slashing Spanish style, and showed Ronald Seabold on the edge of the jungle, in his hand the machete with which he had cut his way through the forest, in his eye the look of a king, and rolling downhill toward the foreground the beginning of a sweep of cleared farmland. If the captain, or the two mates, or the chief engineer, who sat with Joseph at this table, referred in any way to the older Seabold, they were apt to glance aside at the painting, somewhat as though they took it as witness, somewhat as though they were in awe.

In his soul, Joseph denied the picture as a bit of melodrama and reverted preferably to that image which was formed in his memory of the great, dim library, the single pool of light, the white face of a book, the head of Ronald Seabold bent above it.

His curiosity began to grow great, not only about "the General" but about "the Admiral" also. Concerning the former, he gained some information by accident during the dinner, at which he happened to ask: "How old is General Easter?"

"Why, about fifty," said the captain.

"Come, come!" protested the chief engineer, lifting a hand and laughing. "Not more than forty at the most. It was only twenty years ago when he ran the two Degas brothers out of San Esteban, and he was only a lad then; he couldn't have run so fast if he'd been any older—and they turning and trying to shoot, and screeching as he fed the whip into them every time!"

The chief engineer leaned back in his chair and laughed heartily. He had milk-white hair, and a long milk-white mustache that opened like a fish-mouth.

"I remember that day," said the captain. "It happened *after* he came back from Puerto Blaz."

"No, years before that," interjected the first mate.

"I tell you, the scar on his neck was still fresh. I used to wonder how the machete could have cut that far around his throat without slitting the windpipe."

"I remember him for fifteen years," said the second mate, "ever since the storming of San Esteban City; and he's always looked just the same. He's about forty-five."

"He seems about that," said Seabold.

"Oh, he seems about that to you, does he?" asked the captain in a curious voice; and all talk about Easter ended at once. The barrier had risen and the clan retired with its hero. Seabold was left to think of the great man in his cabin with six empty gilded birdcages hanging from the walls, aswing with the motion of the boat. But more than once, at night, he heard voices from the big forward cabin, singing and chatting merrily.

They had slammed the door in his face so effectively that he never expected to open it again, but on the last day, as he walked down the deck, he saw the general standing at the door of his cabin to take the slight headwind which the movement of the ship stirred up in that hot, muggy air. The general was dressed in red slippers, shorts, and his monocle. His body was very straight and young, touched with little silver scars from shoulders to waist.

"Ah, Joseph," said the general. "How has the voyage been?"

"Quiet," said Seabold. He pocketed his pride to add: "I've missed seeing you."

"That's kind of you," said the general. "But I'm no sailor. Haven't the legs for it. The legs go first, Joseph. Is it really your last trip to San Esteban?"

"It is," said Seabold with a hearty emphasis of distaste. "I like air that's cleaner than this."

"Clean or dirty—don't be the last of anything," said the general. "Be the first, but don't be the last. The first to drink; the first to fight; the first to love 'em, and to leave 'em!"

He laughed. Compared with the white of his body his face was red, and there was a trembling looseness of flesh just under the chin.

"I'll be seeing you ashore," he said, and closed the door.

THE YELLOW mud of the Rio Negro River, San Esteban's principal waterway, was already staining the sea where they saw the low shore. The yellow thickened momentarily as they picked up the sight of trees fringing the higher land; and now the pier was visible thrusting out into the stream, with a streak of white water at the tip. Seabold saw palm trees, shacks scattered about beneath them, and a central nucleus of larger buildings whose two-story faces dwarfed the rest of the structures which comprised the coastal town of Rio Negro. Small boats began to close in toward the ship, little flat dugouts under leg-of-mutton sails. They came alongside, the occupants handling the sails by sure instinct as they stood up and shouted a welcome.

In the distance, a train with a ridiculous little engine at the tail of it backed out on to the pier; a launch put out carrying a huge quarantine flag. From the launch a fat chunk of a man, almost as dark as a negro, was handed up the side of the *Avon*. The captain and a bottle of rum with lemon and sugar beside it received him in the dining cabin.

"Will the inspection take long?" asked Seabold of a sailor.

The half-breed rubbed thumb and fingers together significantly.

"Not long, sir," he said. "He has small pockets. That other fellow has bigger ones. He's the customs."

A larger launch approached, with a dignitary standing in the bows.

"You mean that the customs examination begins while we're still at sea?" asked Seabold, amazed.

"They have their own peculiar ways in San Esteban," said the sailor.

Other boats came out. They were, said Jose, dignitaries of the town, the mayor, the *jefe politico* who governed the district, and others who had given the captain of the ship commissions to execute in New Orleans at a quarter of the price they would have had to pay in San Esteban.

The ship warped slowly into the dock. In the toss and roll of the open sea it had seemed a small boat, but it was a great liner compared with the dingy smallness of Rio Negro. Seabold was still looking at that picture, tarnished by the rain, when a little man, all dry and withered, came to him. The man was so thin that his neck was a mere pole with the head stuck painfully on the end of it.

"You're Joseph Seabold?" he said. "I'm Carpenter Robertson—what's left of him. Glad to know you. I'm having your luggage sent over to the Admiral's house. Had the wire about you a week ago. There's bad news, Mr. Seabold."

He pulled his mouth to one side of his face and turned his head in the opposite direction. "Marigny's in San Esteban," he said.

Seabold said: "Marigny?"

"But you know?" said Robertson, amazed. "Marigny—Universal Fruit?"

"I'm not representing anything," said Seabold. "I'm just making a trip. I don't know anything about the company's affairs."

"Not representing—don't know anything?" cried Robertson. "But I have a wire in my pocket from the Admiral saying that you're in complete charge so long as you're in San Esteban!"

"I? In charge? But what the devil can that mean?" exclaimed Seabold.

"You don't know, eh? Well, we'll both find out before long. Shall we go ashore?"

STILL TRYING to grasp the meaning of this odd news, Seabold said good-bye to the captain and went to the gangplank. He was starting down it when a band began to pump out a sonorous tune, the start of it synchronizing with his first step. As he went on, the music of the band staggered, fell apart; every instrument was out of step with all the rest; and then the voice of Robertson reached him from behind: "Stand still; take off your hat. It's the national anthem!"

As Seabold halted and pulled off his hat, he became aware that all along the pier people were standing stiffly at attention. A squad of soldiers presented arms; an officer, in a uniform brilliant as a flower, kept his sword at a steady salute. In the meantime the band fell into step, the music proceeded with a regular swing again, and on a high, shrill, plaintive chord the song came to an end. Seabold was remembering a translation of the words, running something like this:

The sea kisses her feet;
The clouds pillow her lofty head;
San Esteban, when I think of you
Love suddenly rejoices me.
Among all the nations
I see you enthroned, a queen.

"Have I done a terrible thing?" he asked of Robertson, when he reached the bottom of the gangplank.

"Too bad! Too bad!" said Robertson. "But you're representing nothing. Nothing at all. I'll make it all right."

They got into an automobile, as a cloud of children came scampering and squealing around the machine. He could pick the word "Admiral" over and over out of their speech. Their elders remained at a definite distance and stared Seabold up and down with a deep distrust.

The old engine of the automobile started with a roar, but a yell from the entire throng, a pealing outcry that seemed to come from one vast throat, covered the noise of the engine. There was something waving in every hand, handkerchiefs, hats, sticks, flowers, and Seabold looked back to see that a tall figure, splendid in flawless whites, stood at the head of the, gangplank, lifting his white Panama, waving it right and left, bowing a little from time to time in acknowledgment of this tremendous welcome.

On the outskirts of the crowd waited a phaeton with two white horses. Under its canopy of white lined with green silk sat a girl, clapping her hands, laughing, crying out. She was so lovely that Seabold wanted to halt the car and stare at her. Then her glance turned from General Easter toward him. Her hand-clapping almost ceased. She regarded him up and down without concern, and laughed a little as she turned back to swell the reception of the general.

Seabold realized that he had been leaning forward with his weight on one hand, as though he were about to leap from the machine. He settled back against the cushions. His face was hot, but he swore only to himself.

"Who's that?" he asked of Robertson.

"She's our favorite tropical disease; everybody catches it," said Robertson. "Mary Cosgrave. When the Admiral moved into San Esteban, her father had to move out."

"You mean that Ronald Seabold bought him out?"

"Bought? No. Not exactly 'bought.' Moved is a better word. Moved him out..."

SEABOLD DREAMED that he was caught in a quicksand which rose to his lips, to his nostrils, and wakened to find himself involved in a smell of dust and the folds of his mosquito netting. When he got out of the tangle and sat up on the edge of the bed, his face was wet, his pyjamas damp and wrinkled. The last of his dream still worked uncleanly in his mind as he looked at the downpour beyond the window. It shut out the mountains of the interior and gave a false perspective to everything in view. That view consisted of three dripping palm trees and a scattering of chickens who went about scratching and pecking in spite of their wet feathers. A child, naked to the waist, his black hair sluicing down over face and neck, went by on a donkey, bumping the ribs of it with his heels at every stride. Seabold went gloomily into the bathroom for his shower.

As he scrubbed he took note of his body—a little scrawny about the neck and chest, a bulge of soft fat coming above the hips now, and the knees sticking out from the skinny legs. Mysteriously it had made a good football machine, but as he looked down at himself he felt the world's derision like a pointed finger. This cursed San Esteban was building up an inferiority complex in him.

Three days would be enough for this trip. Three stifling days, and after that he could get back to the clean air of the North.

Seabold, at the breakfast table, was still digesting this gloom when two notes came for him. He read:

My dear Seabold:

May I see you? And will you let me know when I may call? Or shall I have the pleasure of receiving you in my place?

Sincerely yours,

James Princeton Easter.

P.S. It was rotten luck for me to be laid up all the trip down. I'm no good as a sailor.

J.P.E.

The rain, which had fallen to a drizzle, rushed back over the house again. Seabold looked up and noted a water stain on the ceiling, gradually spreading, with a fringing of visible drops.

The second note was very similar. It asked him in the most polite terms to call at his earliest convenience. "There is a matter so extremely important that I wish to talk over with you, that I was on the point of coming myself in the place of this note. But it is a rash thing to disturb a man too early in the morning, in a hot climate. If you are up to it, however, won't you drop in on me, and as soon as possible?"

It was signed, "Marigny."

Joseph Seabold had seen that dark face in the North, he knew the man was the greatest enemy and rival of Ronald Seabold; and in fact he could no more resist the invitation than he could have resisted Satan. He put on a cloak against the rain, a big oiled silk that covered him from head to foot, and let a *mozo* of the house direct him to Marigny's place. The face of the servant turned sober when he heard the question. He looked twice at Seabold. He was so suspiciously interested that he almost forgot which way to point.

It was a hard downpour. The rain dropped like skirts from the clouds; it turned Rio Negro into a dingy, flat picture, about to be washed from the canvas. So he came to the house of Marigny with his head down and with barely a glance at the squat length of it. The servant knew him and addressed him by name. Seabold faintly tasted the joy of a vicarious glory as he was shown into a room where the masks of half a dozen jaguars gaped or grinned at him from the walls.

"Señor Marilyn—he shot these?" asked Seabold.

"With a revolver, señor. He finds a rifle too sure," said the *mozo,* and took himself on whispering straw sandals out of the room to call the master.

SEABOLD, AT a window, saw through the running water on the glass as in a river how the garden outside was beaten by the storm. Sodden patches of yellow, of white, of crimson or purple lay on the ground where shrubs had been stripped of their flowers. When someone entered the room he turned quickly about.

It was not Marigny, but that Mary Cosgrave who had laughed at him with such a cool impudence the day before. He remembered what he had been told of the way Ronald Seabold had "moved out" her father from his holdings in San Esteban, and he was surprised by the smiling cheerfulness with which she came to him, holding out a hand.

"I didn't expect to find you in the enemy's camp," she said. "I'm Mary Cosgrave, Mr. Seabold."

"I know," he said, shaking hands.

"About everything?" she asked. "The old war, and all of that?"

"I've heard that Ronald Seabold was pretty rough," he answered. "Is everyone that way, down here?"

He looked straight at her and she admitted this examination.

"I was being contemptible yesterday," she replied. "Is that what you're thinking of?"

"Well, I made an ass of myself, didn't I?" asked Seabold. "Prancing along while they were playing their national anthem, and all that?"

She laughed in a friendly way that put her on his side.

"I saw Carpenter Robertson catch you on the gangplank," she said. "He must have had a few terrible words to say... You know how patriotism is down here. It's like a new coat, and all the natives like to keep it brushed up bright and clean."

He followed with a *non sequitur,* saying: "I don't know much about all this business down here, but Carpenter Robertson says that you have quite an axe to grind."

"I haven't left the place for three long years," she answered. "If one can't plot, one can always counterplot; that sort of thing, you know."

"Three years? Three years?" he repeated.

"Yes, that's true."

"But you're not soggy, like the others. You're brown and clean."

She put her hand to her face in a perfectly unconscious gesture;

yet he knew that everything about her was conscious, arranged, planned beforehand, as no doubt her visit to the Marigny house at this exact hour had been scheduled.

She was saying: "Yes. I have a tough skin; I was born in San Esteban, you know, and perhaps that makes a difference. I'm almost mosquito proof, and the snakes won't bite me..."

Then Marigny came in. His eyes and the unhealthy sallow of his face so held Seabold that the man seemed to drift across the room toward him without visible means of locomotion.

"You two know each other?" asked the girl.

"We know each other," said Marigny, taking the hand of Seabold in a lean paw. "We met—in the North—years ago."

He spoke slowly. He put in the pauses, as though he wanted more time for his eyes to get a hypnotic grip on the brain of Seabold.

"I have to run away, I suppose. I'm not important if Mr. Seabold is here, am I?" asked the girl.

"No, you're not important. Run away," echoed Marigny.

She said good-bye to Seabold.

"I hope we'll stay friends long enough to know one another," she said, and disappeared into the hall.

MARIGNY REMARKED: "The rain—does it confuse you?"

"Maybe a little," said Seabold.

"Sometimes it confuses the minds of people who are new to the tropics. Take this chair where you can watch the water ran on the windows. When you have the rain to see, you don't feel that the weight of it is about to crush in the roof."

Seabold sat down. Marigny said: "What I want to do is to talk business. Now that the Admiral is very sick and you are to be his heir..."

"The Admiral? I?" said Seabold.

"You know that he's very sick, don't you?" asked Marigny.

"A little down, that's all," said Seabold. "Oh, he's the tough hickory. He bends but he's never broken."

He read in the eyes of Marigny a comment that was not spoken. Marigny went on in his soft, steady way, always finding out more with his eyes than with his ears:

"Of course the Admiral never would talk business with me. It was a point of honor with him. To sell out would have been a personal surrender. To sell out to the Universal Fruit, at least. But you have no interest in bananas or San Esteban, and I want to know if you would be interested in talking over a sale."

"I would," said Seabold, instantly, for the man had uttered his wish. "But..."

"Well?" said Marigny. "Are you a little irritated because I presume to know a part of your mind?"

He lighted a cigarette without offering one to Seabold; and yet that did not seem a discourtesy, for it was apparent that Marigny's mind was abstracted from ordinary gestures in order to pour itself without stay into the question at hand.

"I'm not irritated," said Seabold. "But I feel that I'm overmatched. You know too much about all this."

"I don't pretend to want to conclude the bargain today," said Marigny. "I intend a fair price, also. A fair price to you would be a good thing for us, anyway. It would make our monopoly absolute. We would profit a great deal by that. We rule everywhere except in San Esteban. Those are my cards. I put them on the table face up. Do you care to play out the rest of the game with me? I mean, when the time comes?"

It seemed to Seabold that the man was a ghoul, already drinking up the last vestiges of life in the Admiral, reducing him eagerly to a senseless ghost.

"Suppose everything you say turns out true," said Seabold. "Suppose that I *should* step into all this business..."

"To you, nothing but bananas and money."

"To the Admiral, it was the breath of life, also."

"The Admiral," said Marigny, "was a very stubborn man."

The use of the past tense killed the Admiral like a bullet.

"A fellow never knows until the time comes," said Seabold. "I think what you say may be right. But suppose that I step into things; suppose that I like the fight; suppose it seems to fit my hands like gloves of my own making. I don't know."

"Is that where you stand?" asked Marigny.

"That's where I stand," said Seabold.

"Then we've talked as much as we should at this moment," said Marigny, and rose. "I know you have a good many things to do."

He took Seabold to the front door.

"I hope I haven't been abrupt and rude," said Seabold.

"Not a bit. Can I send you anywhere?"

"I'm going only a step, to General Easter's house."

"Good morning, then."

Marigny went back into the room of the jaguars and sat down with his hands clasped around one knee. Mary Cosgrave came soundlessly in to him.

She asked: "Well?"

"We have to wait," said Marigny. "He's going to ask Easter. If they combine, everything grows more difficult for me. What do you think about him?"

"My thinking doesn't matter. I know you've taken him apart and weighed the pieces by this time."

"What do you think of him?" insisted the monotonous voice of Marigny.

So she set herself to unravelling her thoughts.

She said: "Well, on the one hand, he has a clean pair of eyes. On the other hand, he's young; he doesn't know anything about anything; he's lazy; he isn't attractive to a woman. Is he to a man?"

"I think he's a Seabold," said Marigny. "I think we'll have to fight."

THE HOUSE of the general stood on a bit of rising ground, a low, squat wall with hardly a window opening in the face of it. The stream of children who had followed Seabold from Marigny's place gathered about him as he paused before the entrance to the house.

"Are you the Admiral's son?" one of them asked.

And another, laughing, with a voice like a crowing rooster said: "Ask your eyes to tell you. *He* is no admiral!"

They ran away a few steps, shouting and laughing again; they began to point at Seabold. In a moment they were sticking out their tongues, and they raised a yell when a servant admitted him to the house.

The general sat in a small *patio* which was glassed in above, and laid out in a riot of flowers, with great climbing vines twisting up the inner walls. He stood up, in whites as immaculate as ever, and took his monocle from his eye as he called: "Ah, Joseph, very kind of you to come... Rosita, this is Señor Joseph Seabold."

He had fallen into Spanish: Rosita in a butterfly radiance of silks rose and made a curtsy before she took his hand.

"Señora Easter..." began Seabold.

"Ah, I am not the señora," she said. "I am only—Rosita!"

"I beg your pardon," he started to say.

"For finding that I am only Rosita?" she said. "No, please. I am quite used to myself. Will you sit here, señor? It is the chair which the Admiral preferred."

He listened to the Spanish, and felt that thought was colored and warmed by it.

"What will you drink?" she was asking.

"I don't drink in the morning," he replied.

"Ah, but you must. It is a custom of the general. Only his enemies leave him without drinking. A little wine with soda? Yes?"

The general said: "The girl would make a good waitress; she

has the knack of putting a stranger at ease, eh? I suppose that I've lifted her too high. And that means she'll fall on somebody's head one of these days. Get him the wine and stuff, Rosita. And a dash of rum for me. A fellow's blood needs to be stirred in the morning or it may stay asleep all day long."

Rosita left the *patio*. The rain drummed on the glass roofing for a moment, then Seabold broke out: "I'm afraid that she knows English, general."

"Of course she does," said the general. "That's half the game to see how she masks her knowing. It's the way to discipline her, too. I clip her wings with a few English sentences, now and then; otherwise she'd be off with the wild geese one of these days... A pretty girl about the house keeps a man respectable, eh?"

"I dare say," said Seabold.

"But the saying is not what counts," said the general. He laughed. "Don't be afraid of the idea. And remember that blondes don't last."

"Why not?" asked Seabold.

"The steam-heat raises hell with their complexions. The only exception is Mary Cosgrave."

"I've seen her," said Seabold.

"Everybody sees her, and always in the distance," said James Easter. "When she comes to Rio Negro, she watches every boat come in."

"That's strange," said Seabold.

"Not at all. She keeps hoping that she'll see a real man come down the gangplank one day; like the Arabian mare that looks into the horizon every morning and hopes to see a real master coming over the edge of the world."

ROSITA CAME in, followed by a fat-faced house *mozo* who carried a tray; steam already had gathered like frost around the bowl of ice. Rosita poured the drinks, and the general leaned back in a chair with his glass.

"Now you can run along, Rosita," he said. "I have to talk about a very serious thing with Señor Seabold. And you know that when I'm with you, I can't think about other things."

She made a curtsy of farewell to Seabold and gave him her smile. The general grinned as he watched.

"Rosita, you're not too pretty to be true, are you?" he asked.

"Ah, no," smiled Rosita.

"As true as gold?"

"Yes. Or as steel," she said.

"Well, run along," said the general, and she left the *patio.* "She has an edge, you see?" chuckled James Easter. "As true as steel, eh? I think the little devil can see in the dark, there's so much cat in her... Now do you mind if I talk business?"

"Not at all," said Seabold, drawing his mind back from Rosita step by step and focusing his attention on Easter.

"I'm stony broke and need five thousand. Can you let me have it?" asked the general.

"Five thousand dollars?" asked Seabold. "Well... I suppose a note with sufficient security..."

"My dear fellow, I haven't a security in the world. I'm the most insecure man you ever saw."

Seabold sipped his wine and soda, puzzled.

"It doesn't sound like business, does it?" he asked.

"No, it doesn't," answered the general, frankly. He felt the length of his whiskers by shoving his fingertips slowly up one side of his pink face. "Maybe it *isn't* business, either."

Seabold said: "I suppose the Fruit Company must be under an obligation to you. But I don't know what steps have been taken toward discharging the debt."

"Debt?" said the general, waving his hand. "The Admiral doesn't owe me a penny. I'd rather take one step with him than three with the Archangel Gabriel. There's no obligation in the world; not in the world."

"If that's the case," said Seabold, finishing his wine and soda. "I don't really see... I mean, it appears to me..."

"I don't blame you in the least," said the general. "Not a bit. Business is business, and I ought to remember the rules. Don't think of this for another moment... But I see you're uncomfortable; so go back about your affairs. Don't let me keep you, Seabold. Go right ahead. Delighted that you dropped in. After all, five thousand dollars is a lot of money!"

"I think that a smaller sum..." said Seabold, as he stood up.

"When the water leaks through the dam," said Easter, "there's no use in a plug that's smaller than the hole."

SEABOLD, TROUBLED, took the way to the office to consult Robertson. The rain was sloshing down all the while in torrents that slanted sometimes into his eyes and blinded him. It seemed to him that one glimpse of a clear horizon would enable him to be twice the man that he was showing himself to be here in Rio Negro, but thought was drowned in this rain, stifled in this muggy atmosphere.

A bell began to boom out slow notes. Other bells joined in a heavy monody, small bells and great, sharp little treble calls, followed by huge bass thunderings. He passed a building which Robertson had not identified for him when they were making their tour of the town the day before. Through the mist he saw a flag run up the staff at the top. Halfway up the flag was stopped and hung there unstirred by any wind. Some blow had befallen the republic, certainly.

When he came on toward the office building and general headquarters of the Seabold organization, he made out the company flag, red and blue, also at half-mast. There was no bell to ring in the place, but in the big inner court stood the gong which announced noon and the end of the day. It was booming now. A *mozo* stood in the rain, thumping the gong at intervals so that before one shivering, groaning note had quite died out, another began. When he looked up toward the windows, he saw dim faces pressed close to the glass as though there was no occupation for all the clerks except to stare down at the beating of the gong in the court.

He got quickly to the office of Robertson. The latter was sitting at a desk with his head in his hands, the fingers taking such a grip at the skull that the hair stood up in tufts.

"What's happened?" asked Seabold.

Robertson dragged down his hands. He had been weeping, yet he was unashamed. He took a great breath, but the voice that followed it was only a trembling whisper.

"Seabold... Don't you know? The Admiral is dead!"

For a moment the word meant nothing to Seabold. He merely watched the tears that still rolled down the face of little Robertson. The expression of that face was one of weary disgust, but the tears told another story.

Robertson pushed a long telegram across the desk.

"It's from Kelvin," he said. "Died in the night, without a struggle. In the night—peacefully—the Admiral! He came to an end like that! There should have been hell-fire crashing around!... He's gone, and he leaves everything to you. You're the sole heir... You're the Seabold Company!"

What Seabold felt was neither gratitude nor wonder, but fear. The long breath that he took drew the cold of it down around his heart.

After a while, he could hear the voice of Robertson, which had been going on for some time: "... and anything may happen. The cat's away, now... good lord, what am I saying?... But it's true. The mice will play, and what they're apt to feed on is the Seabold Company. We'd better see Jack Easter, first of all."

"I've been to him this morning," said Seabold.

"Ah? This morning?"

"He sent a note and asked when he could call, or if I would visit him. I went to him because I thought he wouldn't expect it."

"Did you think that? Good for you! Very good indeed! Tell me how the talk went."

"Why, well enough, except that Easter said he needed five thousand dollars…"

"That's opportune. That's very opportune!" said Robertson. "You let him have it, of course?"

Seabold turned from the window; and it seemed to him that the ghost of the Admiral instantly was standing behind him, outside the smoking pane.

"You see," he explained, "Easter could offer no security…"

"You mean that you *didn't* give it to him?" groaned Robertson.

Seabold could not answer; the tolling bells poured weight upon his soul, and the booming gong in the courtyard sent a tremor through the building.

"I didn't know that was our policy—" he began.

Robertson cut in on him furiously: "Why didn't you come to me, first? If you don't know, why don't you ask? Do you think that you can step into this business and know about it by inspiration or instinct? Marigny—Marigny's started for the capital, San Esteban City, now!"

Here Robertson stopped himself and stared after his angry words.

"I'm sorry," he said.

"It's all right," answered Seabold. "Shall I go back to Easter?"

"Will you do that?" pleaded Robertson. "Go now, for lord's sake. Tell him that you didn't understand; that you didn't realize there'd be no Seabold Company except for him."

"He told me that he'd been paid well for every service," said Seabold.

"He has been. But still he's to be paid. If the air you breathe cost money, you'd lay down the cash, wouldn't you? Get back to him, please! Go now."

Seabold went.

He swung his weatherproofed cloak over his shoulders, and walked back to the house of Jack Easter with the bells of Rio Negro changing tune about him. He no longer could hear the great gong from the Seabold Building, but the tremor, the pulse of it was still alive in him. A sense of disaster and the horrible bells of Rio Negro went with him through the muddy streets.

HE WAS knocking at the door of Easter's house, waiting, knocking again until he could hear the small echo running tiptoe through the interior. No one answered, of all the servants who had been passing like whispers through the rooms when he was here before. He tried the knob of the door. It pushed open instantly. A slanting volley of rain drove him inside, rattling on the floor until he had closed the storm out behind him. In the mirror of the hat rack he saw the dull, watery image of his own face. The weight of the rain fell in crunching blows on the roof, with the monody of the bells increasing, dying, walking nearer again.

The *patio* lay just ahead; the rain drops drummed a thinner and more musical note on the glass of its ceiling, and he went toward this sound. What he first saw from the entrance was an overturned wicker chair with a tray of glasses broken on the tiles. A wine bottle, splintered to the neck, left a wide pool, the margins splashing out like rays from an explosion. Then, sitting cross-legged on the floor against the wall, he saw Rosita, smoking a cigarette on which a long, crooked ash had formed. She looked at him with empty eyes.

"Señorita," he said, bowing. "I beg your pardon for walking in like this but when I knocked there was no answer. May I see the general?"

She puffed at the cigarette. In her eyes there was no sense of understanding.

He knew by some inward stroke of perception what had

happened. It made him stride to the door which opened arching from the *patio*. He shouted loudly: "General! General Easter!"

The rain had withdrawn a little at that moment, so that he could hear his voice making passage through the corridor, losing itself in the rooms beyond. So, by degrees, he realized what had happened. The general was gone, and at once every servant in the establishment had vanished. Rosita was left there alone.

He stepped into the nearest chamber. It was the dining room, but only the furniture remained in it. The shelves for silver, the sideboard, all had been stripped. On the floor lay the two halves of a lace tablecloth, as though hands had fought for it, ripped it apart, and left the worthless fragments.

He thought he could see the picture of the general, tall and cool in his whites, calling the *mozos* of the place together, telling them briefly that he was leaving them, perhaps giving them permission, in lieu of back pay, to strip the house of its valuables.

Seabold went back to the *patio*. The long ash had fallen from Rosita's cigarette, leaving a grey dribble down the front of her dress, which billowed out around her.

"Rosita," he said. "Can you tell me where the general has gone?"

Her eyes remained unaware of him.

He said, desperately: "You must know where he is... Also, I wouldn't like to see you without means—left deserted and therefore if you can tell me where the general may be found..."

He had pulled out his wallet. There was perhaps two hundred dollars in tens and twenties which he laid in a thick sheaf on the lap of Rosita. Some of the top bills slid off the pile and on to the floor.

She was looking up to him at last, and he prepared to see her smile. In fact, the light was gathering rapidly in her eyes, but what she said was: "Gringo dog!"

After that, she became unconscious of him once more, and Seabold felt tied in hand and tongue. He could not with dignity

bend down to reclaim the money, so he left the house without another word.

The rain was good against the heat of his face.

The street had disappeared under running, yellow water. Over the low places of the sidewalk he stepped ankle-deep; and water was squeaking and squeezing inside his shoes when he regained the Seabold Building.

It had come alive since he last was there. Armed men were gathering under the arcade at the left of the courtyard; barefooted fellows were leading out mules that shook their long ears against the rain, little pot-bellied mules turning black in the wet. When he went up the steps, servants, subordinate clerks, came flying down them, brushing his shoulder without a word of apology.

Others raced up the steps from behind and panted past him. And there was fear in every face.

When he reached the offices, he heard a shouting voice and went to it. It was Robertson, standing in the middle of the floor with men about him, yelling out orders in Spanish.

"See the *commandante* and ask him to lunch with me... Carry my compliments to the *jefe politico* and say I beg leave to call on him this afternoon... Tell Captain Binner to come to me at once... Take six men, you, and go through the guns in the armory..."

With every shouted order, a messenger whirled and raced from the room.

It was empty before Robertson turned to Seabold with recognition in his face. He held up a hand to stop words.

"I know," he said. "Everybody knows. The general is gone. Mary

Cosgrave is gone with him or with Marigny. If the three of them put their heads together, the devil will make a fourth at their talk... What are you going to do?"

Seabold sat down heavily. He could hear the water sluicing off his rain cloak still and pattering on the floor. All he could think of was how strange it was that although his shoes were filled with slush, his feet were warm.

"What are you going to do?" shouted Robertson, suddenly. "You're not going to just sit there, are you? Take the train for San Esteban City. Here I've written out instructions. I've got to hold the fort at this end. Get to the city. Find Easter. Tie him up with steel chains to our side of the business, and there's still a hope!"

OF HIS departure from the coastal town of Rio Negro, two things remained forever in the mind of Seabold.

The first was the scene at the train. A crowd had gathered in spite of the downpour, and in the crowd there were women, men and children. They gave back before Seabold to make a living alley that pointed toward the train, and as he went through the passage he was amazed to see the men with one gesture take off their shapeless hats. Voices sounded about him through the dull, endless booming of the bells of Rio Negro.

"God save you and keep you, señor."

"May happiness wait for you."

And then the shrill voice of a child, saying: "I, too, shall pray for the Admiral!"

The second moment of importance occurred just before the train started. Robertson gave Seabold a letter and said:

"Read this on the way up. You have the name, and you've got to show them that you have the blood and the brain too, or we all go down with a crash... Marigny is the devil incarnate."

Seabold looked into the pale, narrow, strained face, all alive and quivering with grief and with desperate energy.

"Robertson," he said, "If I fail—how you'll despise me!" He could not help saying it, though he saw a small shadow of contempt run over the thin face of Robertson, who answered suddenly:

"For lord's sake, Seabold, you have someone more important than all of us to remember. Think of *him*. And good-bye!"

AFTERWARD, AS the train pulled out, Seabold drew from his pocket the letter of instructions which Robertson had written out.
It began with names and with definitions of them.

1. Lennox. A drunkard but a hero. Keep him sober and you can get fine advice from him. Then get him drunk for the fight, if there has to be one, and he'll be a wildcat to the finish.

2. Don Ricardo Rodriguez, our President. The people nickname him the Fox. They always are right. He has a bright, sharp, animal cunning. If you fill his pockets full enough, you can trust what he will do with his hands. No one has faith in him, but he has allowed the country to become prosperous. Most people feel that he simply is putting it in good shape so that he can reap a harvest before he starts for Europe. He was more afraid of the Admiral than of the devil.

3. Agosto Hurtado. They call him the Lion. Again, the people are right. They love him, but they are a little afraid of him. They like to sing songs about him, rather than to vote for him. They don't like his discipline.

4. The General. No one can define Jack Easter. Your cousin knew how to use him. If he wants to blast the entire country apart, he probably has the brains and the way to do it. Nothing will be built on bedrock until the general is back on our side, or dead.

5. Carpenter Robertson, Rio Negro manager. He is nervous. Has been too long in the tropics. Sleeps badly at night and lives weakly in the day. He should be retired, but the fool won't accept retirement. Believe in his honesty more than in his brains.

6. Joseph Seabold. Too young, much too young, not only as a Central

American but as a man. He must have some power because he is a Seabold. God grant that he doesn't begin to use it too late!

The letter ran on as follows:

General Suggestions:

1. See Tom Lennox, get him sober, make him talk. Do what he tells you to do.

2. Make a large contribution to the church, for any reason you can devise. The church is very strong; the priests are a good lot who love their country; and if they can feel that you are enlisted to help San Esteban, they'll give you invaluable influence among the natives.

3. See the *diputados* and the Cabinet Ministers whom Lennox will name to you. He will give you their exact prices also. Let them have the money they will say they need. Also, promise twice as much as you give.

4. Be sure to entertain some of the generals of importance, and study from Lennox the work of them all so that you can pay intelligent compliments. These people all have done a lot of fighting in rags for the sake of glory.

5. Let yourself be discovered doing some secret acts of charity. This will have an immense influence. Visit the leper's house, if you want to. Walk into the widow's shanty with two porters behind you loaded down with fruit and food and clothes. Go back to the beggar you have passed, ask for his story, laugh in his face, tell him he is an immortal liar, and then give him five dollars because you've enjoyed the lie. No matter how alone you may be when you do these things, be sure that the whole of San Esteban will know about them the next day. From now on, you can do nothing without being observed.

6. Dress simply. Learn the national anthem by heart.

7. Listen to what everyone has to say, and take notes as though you considered the advice important. These people all love to talk; they never will desert, a good listener.

8. Keep a fountain of money at hand. Spend two years profit if you have to.

9. Put spies on the trail of Marigny. He or his agents are about, or soon will be.

10. Ask for the matador after the bullfight, and give him a present as big as you please.

I have listed a number of things that occur to me. Tom Lennox will think of others.

Good-bye. Good luck. All the work that we've been doing in San Esteban now depends on you. It may be wiped out in a week if you do the wrong thing.

Faithfully yours,

Carpenter Robertson.

Seabold folded the paper and tried to repeat the contents to himself; to his amazement, almost every word of each injunction remained printed in his mind.

THE TRAIN clove through a green flume of jungle that broke away right and left, now and again, where clearings had been made for banana farms. On these the plants were of varying ages. Some were very small, breaking the black of the mud in precise rows that seemed ridiculous after the tangle of the wilderness; in some the leaves had arched across, interlocking so that there were avenues of shadow beneath, and the huge, green bunches thrust up above the leaves as though they were afloat on a green sea of waves. Many clearings had been given back to the jungle, which reclaimed them in a single year of prodigious growth. For when the blight appeared, there was nothing to do but to surrender the ground and let the rankness of the forest steam the acres clean again if it would.

Where the farms were cleared, Seabold saw the little houses of overseers standing up on stilts, often with ragged huddlings of native huts behind. Through the wet window, through the downpour beyond, he made out men at work, as though at the dim bottom of a lake. He himself was damp in every stitch of his clothing, but that was only perspiration.

Marigny—Universal Fruit—the dead Admiral... He wondered why he had not told Robertson point blank that he was washing his hands of the entire business. Instead, he had allowed himself to be committed to the fight. Perhaps he would find an honorable way to resign from it. In the meantime, he was being led forward at a breakneck pace, like a child running at the side of a grown man and dragged by the hand over high and low.

SEABOLD SAT at the window of the study in the big house at San Esteban City, and listened to the rain that crashed on the roof or made a sound like the rush of a waterfall through the big trees beyond the window. A stately driveway opened through them to the verge of Lake San Esteban, whose waters were grey as dust with the beating of the rain. Mount Oberone was pencilled out to a flat shadow by the storm, and the smoke from its crater was hardly visible. The scene had little depth; it was like a charcoal sketch. There was such faint daylight that the flame of the fire kept a visible dance along the wall. The day was more damp than chilly, but the fire was necessary for its cheerful face. Even so, Seabold preferred the window view through the park and over the lake, to fronting the huge and shadowy rooms which the Admiral had built around the great *patio*. The *patio* in itself was too much like a palace court, in spite of the flowers that swept up over the walls. All things about the house reminded Seabold that the Admiral had been as a king in this land and that his rule had been long.

The old servant who headed the household came in and bowed.

"A courier from President Rodriguez, sir," he said, "has brought a parcel and a letter."

Seabold opened the letter and eyed the flow of polite Spanish that followed.

Jerry said: "We don't stare at the ladies. What the devil do you mean by it?"

Highly Esteemed and Very Honored Señor Seabold:

From the whole Republic, welcome, dear friend, and particularly to the undying friendship of its President.

But I am in two minds with grief and happiness. Grief because your noble and distinguished relative, my life-friend and counsellor, may visit us no more; happiness because you are here to continue the glorious career of Ronald Seabold.

I yearn to have you instantly beside me, but the cares of the day prevent. This evening, however, I beg you to be my guest at a reception at the palace. There, first time I shall have the joy of beholding your face.

I send as a slight token the medal and ribbon of the Order of Manuel Oberone, with which the Republic makes its first gesture of welcome.

I salute you; I embrace you; I await you with impatience.

Farewell for the moment,

Ricardo Rodriguez.

Seabold unwrapped the package and found, in a nest of fine tissue paper, a magnificent golden medal with the name of Joseph Seabold struck into the reverse. The face showed the head of a gentleman whose chief features were a vast nose and sweeping mustaches. That was the hero, the patron saint, the founder of the liberties of the Republic of San Esteban.

He had hardly put the medal away when General Lennox was announced.

A large, red-faced man with pale eyebrows and twinkling little eyes came into the room a moment later, carrying a white coat over his arm and sweating in dark streaks through his shirt. He squeezed the hand of Seabold with wet fingers and, still holding the hand, turned Seabold toward the window light.

"Well... I can see some of him in you," said Tom Lennox. "It smacked me down when l heard about him. I thought the Admiral would go on forever... Damned if I haven't felt like only half a man ever since... We'll have a drink for the sake of old times, won't we, Joseph? For the sake of the times behind us, and the times to come, eh?"

"What shall it be?" asked Seabold.

"What shall it be? What *can* it be except some of that beautiful rum? Some of that glorious old *agua dolce* that hides its head in a cask and thinks happy thoughts for twenty years before it steps into a bottle and shines for us? Some of that Panama *agua dolce* that your cousin kept in his cellar. That's the thing for us, isn't it? It will make you older and wiser... But curse the getting older; I've had too much of that!"

THEY SAT where the firelight touched them with softly withdrawing fingers.

"You're going to the reception tonight?" said General Lennox. "There'll be that devil Marigny of the Universal Fruit. What could bring him into this part of the world? Watch him, my son. Watch him! His look goes through a man's soul like the slide of a knife. Watch him, and let me help you watch."

"I wish you would," said Seabold. "I'm new to all this business. And I need all the help that my cousin's old friends can give me."

"Don't say a word," answered Lennox, and took a good long swallow of punch before he finished the sentence. "I'll watch Marigny for you. I'll watch him the way a hawk watches a brood of chickens. And I'll let you know. He's come here to make trouble, of course. Trouble's in the air he breathes... But then another thing, Joseph; a very unpleasant thing, for me. I have to tell you that I'm held up for a few days. Northern money that didn't come through. So can I trouble you for a couple of thousand, Joseph? Just for the time being."

"Certainly," said Seabold, and took out his cheque book.

When the cheque was written, Tom Lennox folded it and stood up.

"I'm going to go now and put an eye on Marigny," he said. "If he slips away from Tom Lennox, he'll have to slip fast and far; he'll have to do another Houdini... And good-bye, Joseph... We're going to see something of each other. Tonight at the reception, for one thing. They'll all be there. Easter. Mary Cosgrave. Both in town, I hear. That *will* be a party! Good-bye for the moment."

He went off, and left Seabold slowly pacing up and down the room. There was a certain warm heartiness about Tom Lennox that Seabold liked and trusted. The eyes of the man might be small, but they were amazingly bright, and it was not strange that Ronald Seabold had trusted him. General Easter was announced a moment later.

He came in, saying: "How do you do, Seabold... I had a glimpse of Tom Lennox a moment ago leaving your house with the look of old *agua dolce* about him. Was I wrong?"

Seabold ordered more of the rum, as Easter took the very chair in which Tom Lennox had been sitting.

"I saw Mary Cosgrave on the street," said the general. "Pretty! Delightful eh?"

He began to mix a drink.

"She's beautiful," said Seabold.

"Too beautiful to be this far south," said the general. "And here's your health, Joseph."

"My health is good enough, thank you," said Seabold. "I've been learning a good deal. One of the first things I learned was how much you had meant to my cousin, and on account of that I want to tell you that I made a mistake when you asked me for money. If you still…"

Easter raised a hand to stop him.

"That's ended," he said. "I never ask again for money after it's been refused. That's why I come today to pay my respects and have a last friendly chat with you."

"A *last* chat?" said Seabold. "Are you leaving San Esteban?"

"I'm not intending to leave, but I hope to be able to force *you* out… Don't stand up, don't be excited. I'll probably fail. But I intend to put my hand to the work… I've grown stale and dull. The people no longer have any respect for me. The tradesmen in Rio Negro came and stuffed their bills under my nose. When I kicked them out of the house, they threatened me with the law. A pretty pass when there's a law for me in San Esteban, eh? Then I ask my old friends, the Seabold Company, for a trifling advance and I'm refused… With perfect justice, mind you, but refused nevertheless. And the whisper runs the rounds."

"General," said Seabold, "as soon as I learned how much you meant to my cousin, I went straight back to your house, but it was empty."

"Not quite empty," murmured Jack Easter. "I gave the rest of them the right to loot the place in lieu of their back pay, but there was nothing I could do about Rosita except to kiss her good-bye. Talented girl, that Rosita. I'll be rather surprised if she doesn't find a chance to slip a knife into me one of these days."

He finished his drink and stood up.

"You're a good fellow, Joseph," he said. "Good nerve and all that. But because you set the new fashion in San Esteban Republic of refusing me loans, I'll have to get the best of you and in a very public way. I'll have to try to smash the entire Seabold Company. I'm sorry about it, too. But good-bye."

He held out his hand and Seabold took it.

"You don't give a damn, do you?" asked Easter genially.

"No," said Seabold through his teeth.

"Good fellow," smiled Easter, giving Seabold's hand an extra pressure before he let it go. "You'll pick up a bit more knowledge of the country and make a tough man to beat, before long. If I hit out at you, I'll have to hope that the first punches hurt. In the meantime, I have to tell you that day and night I'm your enemy, Joseph, and intend to do everything in my power to damage you. Good-bye, and the best of luck to you... Beautiful rum, that!"

WHEN SEABOLD dressed that evening, he put on the gaudy medal with which the State of San Esteban had just honored him, in the hope that the curious would not ask for what services he was being rewarded. He went down not to an automobile but to a heavy old closed carriage drawn by four big horses in gilded harness. The driver, the footman, the mounted escort of half a dozen armed fellows, made a picture of antiquated pomp in the rain, and it seemed to him that he was being driven back to the year 1870, through a fourth dimension of time. In spite of the deep mud, however, some automobiles were out, their head-lights making great dim cones of foggy white through the rain. At the entrance to the green park in which the palace of the President stood, there was a brief traffic jam. His escort rode forward. Through the carriage windows he could see them rising in their stirrups. Their shouted words moved dreamily into his mind as they tried to make way for "the Señor Seabold," but no one paid the slightest attention. By lurching degrees they worked their way to the entrance.

A moment later he was out of the uproar of the rain and walking through the long halls, the huge rooms of the palace, with a marimba band tinkling somewhere in the distance and making everyone keep step.

Then he was entering a chamber with an arched ceiling covered with paintings of San Esteban—personified as a very lovely and extremely bare virgin—being crowned by Glory and Honor, also in the buff.

He was passing through the doorway as a loud, clear voice announced, "Señor Joseph Seabold!" and heads turned suddenly toward him; voices stopped. The music of the marimba band drew closer. He was aware of a man with a very dark face that was obscured by a large pair of glasses and a broad smile. He barely was able to recognize Don Ricardo, the President of the Republic, coming toward him with both hands extended, grasping the hands of Seabold, drawing him forward, presenting him to a withered lady in a fluffy pink gown that would have gone well on a girl of eighteen. That was the first lady of the land, extending her hand as though she expected the wrinkled knuckles to be kissed.

After that everyone was smiling, but he felt quite a dim figure in the midst of much brilliance. There were dinner jackets or tails on some of the men, but the majority were in shining uniforms and all with their chests weighted down with medals that jigged and flashed as they walked.

There was no nonsense about passing apéritifs on a tray. Instead, the palace was equipped with a bar and one was expected to make good use of it. It was certainly the most brilliant room in the castle, what with the shine of the long bar and the glistening face of the vast mirror that held the images of a thousand bottles with colored labels; and above all there were no less than three chandeliers, cascading fountains of light.

General Tom Lennox, altogether magnificent in yellow and red, took Seabold almost by force into the bar.

"Joe," he said, "I want you to know Mr. Seabold. Our new Seabold... Joseph, this is Joe. He has a whole set of last names, but they don't count. Do they, Joe? Some of them got him into jail, and so he threw the whole batch of them away. Wise fellow, I say. Joe knows everything. Measures your drink the way a tailor cuts your suit. No waste material. Just enough to cover you with a glow and give you a good time… Measure Mr. Seabold, Joe."

Joe was a tall, narrow man with an inexpressibly sad face and a prominent Adam's apple that seemed to give him pain whenever he swallowed. And he was always swallowing, and having his eyes closed and his mouth twisted by the discomfort. His voice rolled up from profound depths, vibrating like the strings of a great bass viol.

"For Mr. Seabold," said Joe, "a martini smooth would be about the right fit."

Painful deliberation wrinkled his forehead as he considered Seabold.

"It was one of the favorites of the Admiral, sir," said Joe, his hands busily mixing. "For you, General Lennox, the usual?"

"Yeah. Just one of the jokes," said Lennox. "He'll build you up till *you* can take 'em, too, Joseph. But for a fellow that's not used to them, one of Joe's jokes is likely to sidetrack the whole train. After the first one of Joe's jokes, you don't laugh again for a month."

"It is rum," said Joe, seriously confiding in Seabold, "decorated with absinthe and other touches. A man like General Lennox…"

He made a considering gesture with both wet hands, as though measuring out for himself a very large globe. Then, contented, he nodded and swallowed with more pain than usual.

"Joe's got second sight," said Tom Lennox. "And he's made me see things plenty of times. Haven't you, Joe?"

He can tell you anything you want to know, after you've had a drink. Put that one down and then ask him."

Seabold put it down and asked: "What made the smooth in that martini. Joe?"

"A little dry sherry, sir," said Joe. "A strange thing that other bartenders haven't thought of it. Sherry and a dry martini are on the same key, so to speak. They are cognate sounds, sir. Will you have another?"

"It's very good," said Seabold. "I'll have another if you'll tell me what lies ahead of me tonight."

"Happiness and pain, sir," said Joe. "Happiness that passes into pain, or pain that passes into happiness."

"Ah, come on, Joe," said Tom Lennox. "Rub your eyes and see a little clearer."

"Something will touch you, sir. Music. Something like music. I can't see any clearer than that."

"That sounds like bunk to me. I'm ashamed of you, Joe," said Lennox. "Ah. Marigny. Marigny! Come here and meet a Seabold."

MARIGNY CAME with his soft slow steps. His face was leaner than ever. He had the swarthy, sunken cheeks of a consumptive. Latins are apt to have that appearance even when they are as durable as brass. As he came up he began to smile a little, took the hand of Seabold, still smiling, nodded to Tom Lennox, and went on out of the room.

"We've met before," he had said.

"That's him," said Tom Lennox. "There's no need of a smart bartender to tell what's coming to Marigny some day. I can see it clear as a whistle. Him on his face, and the handle of a knife sticking out from between his shoulder blades... But he'll have more millions in the bank by that time than there are *dinges* in the whole of Latin-America... Some champagne, Joe. I wanta raise my temperature. Marigny sure has cooled off the air a lot."

Joe, for once, was not available. He stood with his head raised, and a grin of ineffable delight and admiration twisting his face. For a whole breathing space he failed to swallow, and Seabold saw the reason for the alteration—the general himself was entering the bar.

Easter came up to Seabold and shook hands very amiably. Of all the men in the Presidential palace that night, he was the only one that Seabold had seen without ribbon, or medal, or decoration of any sort. There was not a trace of anything pretentious about him, except perhaps the big pearls which appeared in his shirt front. He seemed to feel the eyes of Seabold upon them, for he said at once, touching one of the jewels: "I had these in my pocket when the *mozos* ran off with the rest of my stuff."

"General," said Seabold, "what did you do with those six bird-cages?"

"I put a parrot in every one of 'em," answered the general. "And every parrot had been taught by a greasy old duenna to say, 'Rosita. I love you!'"

"How is Rosita?" asked Lennox. "I'd walk ten miles and swim a river for one glimpse of that girl. All cream and roses, Jack. All cream and roses!"

"She's somewhere out yonder in the mud of San Esteban," said the general, "whetting a knife for me."

Servants came scurrying through the bar to announce that dinner was about to be served. A special major-domo, pale with hurry and sweat and importance, found Seabold and told him that everything must wait for him since he was the guest of honor. As soon as he arrived in the big hall of reception, the President rose, his wife turned her withered smile on Seabold, and he took her into the dining room behind the fat neck and the bristling grey hair of Don Ricardo.

It was like a tropical garden under a strong sun—that vast table of state with the crystal rivers of glasses flowing around it, and the crimson and golden fruits that heaped the centre. The table was so huge that the people at the farther end seemed small. It was a room of mirrors, so that while the guests were at the table, throngs in diminishing perspective along every wall were nodding and grimacing and lifting the bright glasses, while the servants, who streamed back and forth, trod the little images underfoot. Seabold, with that confusion of brilliance under his eye and the heavy importance of Madame Rodriguez on his left, was only vaguely aware of his other neighbor. That was Mary Cosgrave, brown with sun-stain and lovely. She froze a little as she smiled back at him.

IT WAS hard for him to make talk with Madame Rodriguez because all up and down the table eyes were catching at him with barbed curiosity—picking him up, and discarding him, and passing on again. Afterward, when they smiled with one another, he had a disagreeable certainty that they were smiling at him. He wished with all his heart that the dinner would not last long. Madame Rodriguez talked a good deal about "the good Admiral" and how desolate the unhappy news of his death had made her. She talked about finance also, with the practical knowledge of a banker or broker, until she saw that she was far outside the field of her guest. When she was sure of that, she gave him up with a weary smile and turned her attention to the mustachioed general on her left.

The girl said, looking at Seabold with her calm incurious eyes: "What sort of a war are you going to fight down here?"

"War?" asked Seabold.

"It *is* war, isn't it? To the knife, or how? There are still a few little independents that the Admiral permitted to carry on. But they were *his* friends, not yours."

"What do you think I should do?" asked Seabold.

"What do I think? Why, make a clean sweep, of course. That's what I'd try for. Why should you let us live?"

"So far as I'm concerned, there's no war," he answered. "I'm not fighting."

"Not fighting?"

"Not for bananas." He laughed a little. There was no spark of response in her, only a continuation of that coldly impersonal survey. "I know nothing about the business," he added.

"Oh," said she. "Don't you?"

And he was dismissed from her thoughts, a gradually fading

image that left her mind rubbed clean of him in a moment. He was off to a wrong start in this country, plainly, and he would never get in step with the people who lived here; he was sure of that, and the shame that made him perspire also angered him. He was surprised when she said to him a good deal later:

"You are thinking thoughts of war, Mr. Seabold."

"I was thinking what a fool a man seems when he's a fish out of water," he answered.

"Oh?" said she. "I suppose that's true."

This crude frankness forced him to say: "I'd know a lot more about this business of war or peace if I could tell how thick you are with Easter and with Marigny."

"I? With Jack Easter?" she echoed.

"Strange idea, eh?" asked Seabold.

He looked straight at her and had the savage pleasure of seeing her eyes widen just a trifle. But she was unaware that she had betrayed herself.

"Poor drunken Jack!" she said.

That was the total burden of their conversation. The more he set his teeth to find easy topics for talk, the blanker his mind became. His anger increased more than his nervousness. After all, she was like one of those heroines of romance that filled the novels of thirty years ago, lovely girls full of high spirits which they showed by kicking the hero in the face whenever an opportunity showed. The only mystery was why the hero persisted like a dolt in his love and in his service. Women, he decided, are crueler than men because they are smugger.

That wretched meal drew on toward a conclusion before a little whisper passed through the room, not among the guests but through the servants. Then a man in a wet uniform came in, taking big strides, bowed to Madame Rodriguez, and gave a fold of paper to the President. All the talk at the table ended, for obviously casual business would never be permitted to interrupt such an affair as this. Don Ricardo read the message, laid the paper face down and rose from his chair.

Seabold heard Mary Cosgrave murmur: "Now it comes!"

The President said in a good, steady voice:

"My dear friends, I beg you to forgive me, but we have come to a moment of importance to us all... Señor Marigny, permit me to inform you that you are under arrest... General Easter, you likewise are to be placed under surveillance... The well-known traitor who cares nothing for our country except to draw its blood, the five-times rebel against us, has risen again... Hurtado has taken Palos with a handful of ragged poor devils... It is nothing if it is stamped out quickly; but it is my duty to stamp at once... My dear, will you see that everything goes on without further interruption?... Señor Seabold, may I ask a few moments of your time in my study?... Again, a thousand pardons!"

A dozen armed soldiers had seeped into the room. Seabold looked straight down the table at the general, and saw him lifting a champagne glass and drinking to a dark-faced young beauty at his side. The soldiers were behind his chair before he had finished his glass. Marigny had turned about and was speaking to his own armed escort with an air of easy detachment. Everyone at the table took the announcement as though it were a thing of the least moment; only Madame Rodriguez stared before her like a sleepwalker.

THE STUDY of Don Ricardo Rodriguez was a pleasant little room, with books covering the walls and a formidable desk in the centre on the rug. Behind the desk the President was now seated. He half rose to greet Seabold and, dropping back into his chair, he said cheerfully:

"The Seabolds rose with Rodriguez, and now it seems that we will fall together... Try one of these cigars; take this chair and be comfortable, my dear friend. Tomorrow we may be riding mules as fast as we can for the seacoast unless they decide to shoot me against a wall."

Seabold looked into the plump face and could see nothing but smiling cheer in it; yet he knew that there was an entire earnestness behind the words.

"You have your own army; Palos is quite a distance away," said Seabold.

"I have an army," said Rodriguez. "But my people don't like to fight unless their pay is up to date. That's the advantage the revolutionists always possess. Their men fight for hope. My men fight for their salaries. You see?"

"But your treasury…"

"Empty, my dear fellow. Totally empty. You understand how it is. The Admiral must have told you. The men of San Esteban hate taxes and love fiestas."

"If you can't raise taxes, how can you run the country?" asked Seabold.

"Sit down," answered Don Ricardo. "Let me try to explain. We make some money from the customs. We make some more money from small taxes levied on odds and ends. But as a rule we have to wait for people who wish to buy concessions before we can fatten the treasury to any extent. Mining concessions, or land for banana farms."

"Such as Ronald Seabold paid for?"

"Ah, there is the point that involves you with me," said Don Ricardo. "The Admiral often wished to change the *acuerdas* into concessions; I often tried to induce the Congress to vote him what he wanted. But politics are a game of time, and we were just short of the time we needed."

"*Acuerdas?*" asked Seabold.

"They, you see, are merely the Presidential grants," said Don Ricardo; "things which the President of the Republic can give but which also he can take away… Ah, you understand, señor, that it is hard for me to conceive a situation that would cause me to retract those gifts to the Admiral; for he and I were men who worked with two minds but with only a single hand. We were as one in everything that concerned San Esteban."

Seabold said: "I understand it this way: All the banana farms of the Seabold Company are planted on farm lands that don't belong to us; they're only Presidential gifts that can be taken away. The things that can't be retracted are the Congressional concessions."

"You've put it perfectly," said Ricardo, shaking his head sadly. "How I have fought to work the measures through our stupid Congress, but those politicians who call themselves patriots—the scoundrels!—are always ready to make speeches in which they rave against giving away forever the finest lands in San Esteban."

"May I change the subject for a moment?" asked Seabold.

"As you will. Certainly... *Hai!* Are they cheering Hurtado now in the streets?"

HE LOST ten years of fat slowness in getting from his desk to the window. Through the uproar of the rain, Seabold listened to the shouting out of the distance. It seemed to be progressing toward the palace; and he wondered if this room might not become the central stage for one of Central America's musical-comedy revolutions.

Don Ricardo said: "No. That's all right. Some of my own men cheering for the war, because they think it will mean the payment of the arrears." He came back toward his desk.

"I wanted to ask," said Seabold, "why General Easter and Marigny had to be arrested."

"That is simple," answered Don Ricardo. "You see, there are two big fountainheads of money—the Seabold Fruit Company and the Universal Fruit. Revolutions must feed on money. Where could old Hurtado have found the hard cash except from Marigny?"

"If that were the case, why would Marigny be here?" asked Seabold.

"Because he makes the mistake that all clever men may be guilty of. He thinks that he can bluff his way through trouble. Because he feels that all other men are stupid. Perhaps I can show him that he is just a little wrong. Perhaps Hurtado, that one-legged bullfrog, will find himself without support."

The President rubbed the fat of his hands together and his skin chafed audibly, like two pieces of paper.

"And General Easter?" said Seabold.

"There you have the man who doesn't care on which side he fights so long as there *is* fighting," said the President. "So for a few days I see which side he is apt to jump toward. I try to persuade him that it would be better for him to fight at my side than to throw himself toward his old companion, Hurtado."

Seabold asked pointblank: "What would you want from me, Don Ricardo?"

"I speak of a million pesos which is only four hundred thousand of your country's dollars... You see, dear friend, that I am not one of the confiscating villains of which you have heard. And if you give the money, then it is easy for me to win the concessions for you. Ah, this is the very moment for which the Admiral yearned—a time of national danger when he could make his generosity be felt, so that our Congress gladly would confirm all the *acuerdas* I have given to him and transform them into everlasting concessions!"

"Four—hundred—thousand dollars!" murmured Seabold.

"To confirm forever the millions upon millions of dollars worth of rich lands which your company is holding in San Esteban! But without money, my soldiers will sulk like dogs. An army without money is like a body without life. It cannot move. Your cheque in my hands, and I can go before the Congress at once with such a speech that the ears of your opponents will burn with shame.

All of your enemies who have hated your great company, who have won their elections by cursing the foreigners who hold the fairest parts of San Esteban—"

"The company has a great many enemies, then?"

"My dear friend, that is the nature of politics. But how they will have to hide their heads when I go before them and tell them that in time of need you have poured out more than blood for our cause..."

"They will say that I'm simply a practical man trying to hold on to what I own."

"Perhaps in your own country men would say so, but the men of San Esteban have hearts easily touched... I see you are moved, as the Admiral would have been moved before you. I have in this desk a blank cheque..."

"You know, Don Ricardo, that I'm new in this country and don't understand the ways of everything. I'll get the best advice I can, and let you know in the morning."

"There is no time lost. The morning, then. But already I feel hope!"

He followed his guest to the door.

"If people ask why I had to be closeted with you, tell them that we spoke of the Admiral... Some of my generals will be jealous because I've turned to a stranger first, in the time of trouble. But to me no Seabold is a stranger. As soon as my eye fell on your face, my heart was warmed, my son."

THEY WERE dancing in the ballroom as though revolution never had been heard of in the land. In the bar glasses were clinking and winking merrily, and it was here that he found Tom Lennox, a little redder of face than before.

He got Tom to a reasonably secluded corner and said: "Tell me about Hurtado. Is he one of the real people? Is he dangerous?"

"Old Hurtado! Tell you about him?" said Lennox. "Old walrus

with not enough room on his upper lip for a mustache. Agosto Hurtado! There's a man to drink his rum straight and eat raw chilis to wake up his thirst... He knows old Tom Lennox, too."

"Don Ricardo wants support," said Seabold. "Will you tell me how much money he ought—"

"Lemme tell you about old Hurtado," said Lennox. "If you meet up with him just say, 'You know my friend, Tom Lennox?' Then you wait and see what happens. Just say that: 'You know my friend, Tom Lennox?' Why, brother, we've eaten our beans out of the same pot. We've been—"

"It's Don Ricardo that wants—"

"He ain't a drinkin' man," said Tom Lennox. "Waiter, gimme another glass champagne... The trouble with Don Ricardo he ain't a drinkin' man. Now you an' me... I dunno what there is about you that makes me like you so damn much! We're going to have a drink together and then we're..."

Seabold left the drunkard and started out of the bar, past a group that held Mary Cosgrave like a star, she was so shining with happiness. He was a few paces past her when chance stilled the marimba and the dash of rain against the windows, so that he heard her say distinctly: "He won't stay to fight... Bananas aren't worth it... He's running away!"

He stopped and looked back toward her steadily, and she returned the look with a manifest contempt. A tall young English-man in her group came straight up to Seabold.

"Jerry—please!" called the girl.

Jerry said to Seabold: "We don't like Northern manners in this part of the world. We don't stare at the ladies. What the devil do you mean by it?"

His eyes were glassy with liquor, his upper lip thick with it.

"I'll talk with you when you're sober," said Seabold, and left the bar.

Someone was laughing behind him, loudly. That was tall Jerry. Seabold's face was so cold that he knew the white of it.

THE RAIN was ended when Joseph Seabold's carriage took him home; and the wide silence spoke to him, as he felt, of his own shame. The groaning lurches of the old carriage, the stagger and sloshing of the wheels in the ruts tormented his mind, because he wanted to gather his thoughts and examine himself inwardly.

When they came to the entrance driveway of the Seabold mansion, the wheels crunched smoothly over the gravel, but the driver did not put his team to a trot. Instead, he blew three blasts on his horn. Seabold, through the misted windows of the carriage, saw the horn answered by a sudden appearance of lights along the front of the building, the fronds of the intervening palms leaning black across that background. Half a dozen of the house servants were lined up to greet him after the carriage had stopped in the big *patio*. They were all smiles and bows and good wishes until the darkness of his face sobered them; he was glad when they left him alone in his bedroom and he knew that they were glad to be gone from him. There was no one in San Esteban whom he could please. Filibusters of the old school, diplomats, servants, all disliked him, and since his encounter with the tall young Englishman that evening they would begin to despise him, no doubt.

He sat staring at the white mosquito netting which shrouded the bed and under which the Admiral had slept so many times in the calmness of an assured strength, but his thoughts remained back there in the palace of the President confronting the Englishman. He felt that he never had been tested before. Boxing gloves in a gymnasium with an instructor or a friend were one thing; personal opposition in a strange country was quite another. He remembered how cold his face had been afterward, and could not tell whether it had been caused by the Englishman or by the laughter that had followed him. It was not a matter of fisticuffs, of course, for that sort of thing was impossible; it was merely a question of out fronting a hostile pair of eyes.

Robertson's hands were full of telegrams. "Hurtado's raising the devil," he said.

He took off his clothes and went to bed. The mosquito song kept him from thinking anything to a conclusion. All he could remember was the time he had heard a friend say about another friend: "Champ is all right. We all like Champ, of course. But some people say that he's just a little yellow."

Seabold sat suddenly up in the bed, nauseated. But the answer to his own self-question was only the thin whining of the mosquitoes. He lay back. The bedclothes were damp and hot. Sleep came over him like a miserable drug.

CARPENTER ROBERTSON was there in the morning, his eyes big and tired in his scrawny face.

He had taken a social train the instant word came over the wire of the revolt of Hurtado. He had with him the first counter-effort of the President, a handbill hastily struck off the press that showed pictures of Agosto Hurtado in profile and in full face. Hurtado had the common look of a peon, a broad chunk of a face, heavy in the jowls, and with a huge spread of mustaches which were not gathered into points at the side but fanned out into an unkempt brush. Don Ricardo offered fifty thousand pesos, which meant twenty thousand of the good Northern dollars that the President admired so much, for the apprehension of the traitor, dead or alive.

Robertson knew everything. He said:

"Hurtado made a fool of himself. He hit out before he had Easter and Marigny beside him. Otherwise there would be hell to pay. With that pair in his hands, Don Ricardo ought to be able to handle this affair pretty easily."

"Marigny wanted to be captured," said Seabold.

"Wanted? Are you out of your wits?"

"I saw his face at the moment of the arrest... You can call it a mask he was wearing, if you please. But I tell you that he was not displeased."

"Come, come!" answered Robertson. "You can't pretend to do what no other man in the world can manage—read Marigny's mind. I've seen the roulette wheel take fifty thousand from him in five minutes, and he simply seemed amused, like a bull terrier when it sees a chance for a fight. No, no! Don't tell me that Marigny is pleased. Why the devil should he be pleased?"

"I don't know," admitted Seabold.

"Neither do I," snapped little Robertson, dismissing the idea. "Now tell me how much money Don Ricardo wanted from you."

"You'd know that, would you? That he'd ask for money?"

"Joseph, what is the Seabold Company here for except to make contributions when the pinches come? Of course he'd ask you for money. But how much?"

"A million pesos."

"Four hundred thousand dollars? The dirty, contemptible, blood-sucking leech! Four hundred thousand!"

"Shall I offer him a quarter part of that?"

"No, you've got to give him what he asks. The whole of it. There's no other way. The whole of it... The Admiral—he wouldn't have dared to look the Admiral in the face and ask that much. What did he say to you?"

"He said the soldiers were behind in their pay, and that the treasury was empty."

"Of course it's empty, and Don Ricardo has three or four millions of the treasury money cached away safely in Paris banks. But a million pesos! You gave it to him, of course?"

"I told him that I'd have to wait until morning and think it over and—"

"My lord, why did you do that? We're the jackals and he's the lion. We can't afford to bargain with him. All you've done is to make him realize that we don't trust what he says. Joseph, I never should have let you come up here alone, but how could I have guessed?... Go to him as fast as you can and take the chequebook with you. He'll want a million and a half, after he's had a chance to think his needs over all night long... But you have to give him what he wants. There's still money in your New York deposits. Go on, Joseph, and get the dirty business done with!"

THAT WAS why Seabold went back to the Presidential palace

with a feeling that he was under the whip. He found San Esteban City a vastly changed place, now that the rains had let up.
The mountain which smoked beside the great lake had stepped
leagues nearer during the night; with its smoke streaming behind,
it gave a foolish semblance of being under full steam for the little
city. And all the town was out to enjoy the blast of the sun. Thick
mists smoked up from the wet of the streets. In the gutters water
was still gurgling. The atmosphere was of a greenhouse thickness;
the mere labor of breathing started sweat.

His carriage left him at the Presidential entrance. A yellow-
faced servant took him to a chocolate-colored secretary, who
ushered him into a waiting-room where officers in service
uniforms that looked surprisingly drab and efficient were taking
their ease and talking with much laughter.

He waited there a half hour with the certain knowledge that he
was being disciplined, because the insolent, smoky eyes of offi-
cialdom constantly looked askance at him and then interchanged
grins with one another. Then a door opened and a big, fat fellow
on the threshold was saying: "Now, Mr. Seabold, if you please."

So he went into the study, to find the President standing in front
of a big map that covered half of one wall. He was sticking pins
in it, pins with blue or red tiny pennons attached to them. When
he heard Seabold's voice, he said, absently: "Ah, yes—my friend."

Then he turned with a tired smile and gave his hand languidly.

"A bad business!" he said. "I'm glad that you didn't make up
your mind last night. I spoke too quickly. There's poison in the
veins of my country, Señor Seabold, and we need strong medicine to fight it... I said a million pesos last night. Bah, it would
not cover half the needs!"

He made a gesture with both hands.

"I'd ask for twice that much, because I trust the generosity of
your company as a child trusts its father. But shame prevents me. I
tell you, my dear friend, that I could weep for shame when I think

that the President of a free republic has to turn abroad to find the sinews of war. But we are poor. Ah, the curse of poverty! I turn my head away and ask like a beggar for a million and a half pesos… Refuse me, scorn me, but I must ask what the country must have!"

He did not, in fact, turn his head away, but with an eye as bright as the eye of a parrot, he studied Seabold. And all that Seabold could think of was that Carpenter Robertson had struck the nail so exactly on the head. He had known to a penny just how the demand would increase, and a profound disgust stifled Seabold as he drew out his chequebook.

"You can cash it here?" asked Seabold. "Your banks can cash it?"

"They can—they will—they must!" said the President. "Ah, when I go before the Congress this very morning and tell them of what you have done! They will know then whether or not I have found them a friend for our country. Señor, for you this is a glorious act of generosity. For me, it is a triumph of faith!"

But Seabold heard, through the unctuous voice, a triumph that was purely one of laughter. He got from the official presence as fast as he could. Yet he knew, on the way back to his house, that he had not done the thing properly. He should have declared that the vaults of the company were swept bare by making this contribution. He should have vowed that it was only because his heart bled for San Esteban as for his own native land that he had been willing to make such a sacrifice. For he began to see that a lie must be confronted with a lie, and even though the false stamp is apparent, the coin will pass current in some mysterious manner.

HE WAS six hundred thousand dollars more committed to this country than he had been the day before, he realized grimly as his carriage returned toward his house, the smoke of the volcano pointing a dark flag down the sky.

A boy on a mule went trotting by, his voice shaken to bits as he sang:

Dirty face, dirty face
I will wash you in the fountain of my love:
Shameless one, shameless one...

That was like San Esteban, he thought—a dirty face, and who could have love for the place? But as the thought came to him, he relented from it a little. That flag of smoke in the sky, and the golden strength of the sunshine, and the big blue mountains heaped into the sky, made him think of the Admiral in new terms. That conqueror would not have striven for a conquest that was not worth the making.

When Joseph reached the house, he found little Carpenter Robertson pacing up and down under the great vault of the library, with the brilliant flash of the lake showing like touches of quicksilver through the trees beyond the windows. Robertson's hands were full of telegrams.

"Old Hurtado is well up from Palos," he said. "And he's raising the devil—and a big army—as he goes along. How much did Don Ricardo want?"

"You knew the figure to a penny," said Seabold.

"And you refused it again?" exclaimed Robertson. "Don't tell me that! It will be two millions the next time."

"I didn't refuse. I paid."

"But you can't have paid!" shouted Carpenter Robertson, the cords of his thin neck standing out with his vehemence. "Of course you can't have paid. Heavens, man, you're still back there telling him that it's more money than you have in cash—that you've got to beg, borrow and steal it, that only personal devotion to his dirty self induces you—and he's sweating and making promises of new concessions, new *acuerdas*..."

"I couldn't bargain," said Seabold simply, "because if I'd had to spend another five minutes with the hypocrite, I would have told him to go to the devil and take his country along with him."

Robertson, for a moment, eyed him stupidly. Then he said: "Well, all right; it's done. That's all... It's done! You gave him the cheque? He'll get the cash for it by wire. Then we'll see... I've got to be off and buzz around the town and see what's happening. How do the people look?"

"Happy," said Seabold.

"Marigny! What's Marigny doing in the prison? What's he thinking?" murmured Robertson. "I'd give ten years of life to be inside his mind for a moment."

"He's not beaten," answered Seabold, remembering the dark, sneering face. "Whatever is true about him, he's not beaten."

"We'll see," answered Robertson, and left the house in his usual hurry.

His last injunction was: "Just stay here where I'll know how to find you if a pinch comes... I don't like all this. I don't like anything about it, except that Marigny is under Don Ricardo's thumb. That's the only blessing in the business."

Later that day, a clashing of steel brought Seabold to a window and he saw, in the court, a pair of *mozos* fencing with heavy machetes. They worked with the skill of trained foilsmen and the ferocity of tigers. The quick blade-work dazzled the eyes of Seabold as he watched, and he carried back to his chair a rather different conception of the men of San Esteban. The books and the newspapers cheapened them beyond comparison; and still there was the fact that the Admiral had chosen to live so many years in the country. Not altogether for money, perhaps. It was impossible to define the Admiral in terms of money entirely.

HE HAD no word from Robertson by late afternoon, so he went out in a powerboat for a spin on the lake. It was the only way of finding coolness after the thick, close heat of the day. He sat with his face to the imperial purples that had gathered around the mountains; he was still on the water when the horizon turned green, the sunset spread into quick darkness, and the stars came down close through the sky.

The motorboat was close to the private pier by that time, and all the little fishing boats were scurrying for the shore, when the man in the bows jumped up and shouted: *"Ah hai!* All dark! The house has no eyes!"

It was perfectly true that the house of Seabold was not glimmering at them from behind its screen of trees. And he heard the helmsman-engineer mutter: "By heaven, isn't one death enough? Is there a plague?"

The two men went up with him from the pier. They were close under the dark wall of the house when a light shone from the library window, and then the voice of Carpenter Robertson was crying out: "Seabold! Hello! Joseph! Oh, Joseph!"

Here the two boatmen paused, making a sudden halt. Seabold answered with a shout and hurried through the side entrance to the library, where Robertson was waiting in the middle of the room, with his hands gripping the back of a chair that covered him almost to the shoulders. He made Seabold think of a head on a tray, a head fresh from the guillotine, the eyes of the little man were so blank.

"Why's the house so empty? Where has everyone gone?" demanded Seabold. "I took a spin on the lake, and then…"

"You might as well have dived into it and never come up again," said Robertson in a dead voice. "You haven't heard?"

"Heard what?"

"They're shouting it through the streets. You're done. Marigny's in with Universal Fruit, and you're out. Out forever!"

"All right," said Seabold.

"All right?" shouted Robertson. "Do you understand what I'm saying? The double-crossing dog of a Don Ricardo went before his Legislature this afternoon and told the deputies that there was only one thing to do in the emergency, with Hurtado marching on

San Esteban and growing stronger every moment... The one thing was to ally themselves with the great Universal Fruit Company, because the only Seabold was a witless boy!"

Seabold took a chair.

"Go on," he said. "Marigny is out of prison and in the saddle... The deputies did everything that Don Ricardo wanted?"

"They voted the Seabold Company out and the Universal in, and they did it with cheering... Yes, Marigny is out of prison... You were right about one thing. I thought that the snake was being swallowed by San Esteban; instead, the snake was doing the swallowing... And heaven deliver me from the lying sound of the Spanish tongue forever!"

"So even the servants ran out on me?" asked Seabold.

"They ran out. Of course they ran. They're kissing the foot of

Marigny now, I suppose. They ran out, and you'll be on the run before morning, if you know what's best for you."

"What's happened to Mary Cosgrave? What's happened to her father's claims?" asked Seabold.

"How did you guess at that? Why, the Cosgrave Company is brought to life, as an ally of the Marigny outfit. They get some large holdings. Large? Well, only a drop in the Marigny bucket, but enough to make her rich for life. Enough to make her feel that she's even with the Admiral for the old days... Three days ago everything on an even keel, and now no keel at all!"

"I seem to have thrown everything away," said Seabold.

"You, or some black devil of bad luck... I don't know. I'm going crazy. We'll try to get down to the seacoast together. I don't know. They may be glad to get rid of us. Or else they may simply stand us against a wall and shoot us down... Will you pack what you think you need for the trip down the river? We won't dare to use the railroad."

"Jack Easter," said Seabold. "What's become of him?"

"Easter? Why, there's only one thing that they'd do with Easter. There's still old Hurtado in the field. Marigny has double-crossed him and gone over to fat-faced Don Ricardo. That means that Hurtado will be without money, which means that he'll soon be through if there's a good general to oppose him. And Marigny and Don Ricardo have found the good man."

"Will Easter fight for them?"

"He will," said Robertson.

"I don't believe it," said Seabold.

"Think it over again. Who was it that slapped Easter's face a few days ago? Five thousand dollars! You wouldn't let him have five thousand dirty dollars!"

"That's cost me six hundred thousand in the meantime," said Seabold.

"And now it's cost you all the rest," answered Robertson.

"I don't think so," said Seabold. "I don't think that Easter will fight for 'em. He was too long on our side."

"Will you believe," cried Robertson, "when I tell you that Easter's already *generalissimo?* Does that make any sense to you? When I tell you that Don Ricardo marshalled a square of two thousand soldiers and gave Easter a sword and the whole command? Does that convince you? I've only come from the seeing of it! I saw the President pin the épaulettes on the shoulders of Easter. Now do you believe me?"

"No," said Seabold, "I don't believe."

"What the devil are you talking about, man?"

"I can't tell, exactly. But there's too much lion in Easter. He can't fight for a rat like Marigny."

"You'll find that out afterward," said Robertson. "Now we start for the coast. We start for Rio Negro, and we can pray to God all the way that we're not caught."

"You go ahead," said Seabold. "You've done your best, and it wasn't good enough. I was too much in your way. You go ahead, Robertson, and take care of yourself."

"And you?"

"I'm staying here," said Seabold.

"There'll be a bloody, pillaging rabble here in half an hour," said Robertson. "What are you talking about?"

"I'm telling you that I'm staying here... I never cared for this whole business before, but now I rather like it."

Carpenter Robertson came out from behind his chair for the first time.

"Ah, I see," he said. "You think you can play at being the Admiral, do you?"

"I think I can play at being myself," said Seabold.

THERE WAS NOT even a stable-boy remaining in the big establishment. Seabold got into riding clothes and picked out in the bar a serviceable-looking mule; in the slosh that filled the streets he wanted something better than the footing of a horse beneath him.

Carpenter Robertson came out with a flashlight and stood helplessly beside him as he cinched the saddle on the mule, digging his knee in to make the brute stop puffing his belly. Robertson said: "What's the good, Joseph? What can you do? Where can you go?"

"I don't know," said Seabold. And he swung himself on to the back of the mule. It hunched under him as though ready to buck.

"If you don't know, why start out in the dark?" asked Robertson.

"Suppose that I could pick up the trail of the Admiral?" asked Seabold.

"The trail? Of the Admiral?" asked Robertson. "You don't understand. He was white magic, in this country. You can't do what he did."

"If I can find the way he travelled, I'll try to take my own steps," said Seabold. "Where will General Jack Easter be staying?"

"In La Casa del Rey—that big old hotel. Listen to me. You can't go to Easter."

"He's my starting point," said Seabold.

The *patio* of La Casa del Rey was dry by this time, and over the cobbles people were trooping continually. All around the court were iron rings fastened into the old stone pillars, and everything from mountain burros to blood horses were hitched to the rings, switching their tails and shrugging their skins vainly at the mosquito hordes. Barefooted peons stood about, and soldiers with shoes or without, and now and then some personality in medals and gay uniform passed under the lights through the entrance arch. Joseph lighted a cigarette and went into the hall, which was the central swarming place of the hive. He met the big Englishman and Mary Cosgrave coming out. It was suddenly easy to look the man straight in the eye, which was a clean, pale blue.

"There he is with his tail between his legs," said Jerry. He said it loudly, with his glance steady on Seabold.

The girl glanced up at him angrily, saying: "Don't do that! Don't be this way, please!"

Something about her attitude gave Seabold more inches. He found his voice coming smoothly as he answered: "I don't know what you want—a Tom to your Jerry? A fist fight? What do you want?"

"I'll take whatever—" began the Englishman.

The girl said: "Jerry, be still!... I'm ashamed."

That last was to Seabold.

He answered her: "Don't you be ashamed. He's helped me to grow up."

He felt her glance pulling after him as he went on into the crowd. There was such a queer happiness in him that he seemed light of foot. He had turned a new page in his life, and the story in it was changed without warning.

"I want General Easter," he said to a hotel servant.

"Ah—all the world wants him—in there," said the man.

The hotel was a sprawling affair with the best rooms on the ground floor. One of the doors stood open, with a pair of soldiers blocking the way. They had bright steel bayonets on their rifles, and new uniforms, and bandoleers of cartridges across their bodies as though they were already in the fighting field. The room behind them was crowded with waiting people of all sorts.

"I want to see the general," said Seabold.

"Name?" asked one of the pair.

"Seabold."

"Ha!" they grunted together. One put out a hand toward Seabold's arm but drew it back again without touching; he merely rolled significant eyes at his companion, who nodded and hurried away through the waiting-room.

"Who comes with you?" asked the remaining guard, with a worried look up and down the bustling of the hall.

"I come by myself," said Seabold.

"God will again save me!" muttered the soldier, with wonder opening his eyes.

His fellow guard returned and nodded. "You come behind me," he said.

He led the way across the next room, shouldering rudely through the crowd.

Someone said in clear English, from a corner: "That's Seabold now. The fool's dead and doesn't know it."

Here the door of the next chamber pushed open. A servant on the threshold was calling out: "Gentlemen—friends—the general can see no other people. He prays you to wait till the morning. And he drinks to your health and begs you to drink to his in the name of Saint James..."

Three more *mozos* came sweating through the same doorway, one with a tray of chattering glasses, two more with buckets that held iced champagne. The people in the waiting-room began to laugh and cheer: *"Viva* Easter! *Viva* the general! The good days are coming back to us!"

"Here is the Señor Seabold," said the soldier.

The fellow on the threshold grunted, stared, loosened his jacket at the throat. "Well, of course! Of course this one!" he said. His grin had begun before the tail of Seabold's eye was past him. The door shut heavily behind; the lock turned in it with a faint screech of rusty iron.

IT WAS a big old room with the four-poster bed partially shut away behind a great screen of featherwork, all glossed over with the brilliant silk of hummingbird plumage. A marble-topped table held the place of central honor on crooked, gilded legs, with a chandelier of crystal pendant above it and throwing dim images of brightness into the polish of the stone. There were tall red curtains by the windows, like streaks of hot noonday; and between a pair of these curtains, lounging in an easy chair with bucket of ice and long-necked bottles, was General Easter, just unbuttoning the official dignity of his coat.

"Ah, there's Joseph!" he said, and got himself to his feet.

"I said there was to be nobody else," he told the soldier.

"Yes, my general," answered the fellow. "But I knew..."

He pointed to Seabold with the palm of his hand, offering him like a gift.

"Go away, then," said Easter. "And sit down here, Joseph. How does it go with you? No, that's the wrong thing to ask. Everything goes like the devil with you... *Hai,* Jose! Pull off my boots and bring me a pair of slippers."

A *mozo* came with bare feet whispering over the floor, kneeled to draw off the boots and offer the slippers. Jack Easter clasped a stockinged foot in both hands.

"Once when we were taking a whack at Palos on the run," he explained, "we found that they'd stuck the ground full of sharpened nails. I did the finding out by stepping on one of 'em; I'd worn out my boots a week before. That damned nail went all the way through; I could hardly hobble to the palisades. Afterward I thought that there would be blood-poisoning, but I got an old Indian doctor and he soaked it for three days in rum. Joseph, if rum is good for a man's foot, think how good it must be for his belly! Will you have some now, or would you rather just blot up some of this Rhine wine?"

He allowed the slipper to be placed on his foot, and waved the servant away. Two more armed men waited motionless at the farther end of the room. Easter appeared not to notice them. Seabold took a glass of the cold wine and sipped it. It was a good Rudesheimer, soft to the tongue, with multiple overtones against the palate.

"Shall I talk now?" asked Seabold.

"Do you have to talk?" asked Jack Easter. "Won't drinking be enough? I've been talking so long to the damned *politicos* that my brain's gone with them."

"I know," said Seabold. "You don't like 'em, do you?"

"Not a bit."

"Neither do I," said Seabold, and took another drink.

He seemed able to watch the pink face of the general without keeping his eyes upon it.

"Politics—and bad gin—rotting the soul out of the world," said the general. "What you say, Joseph? Rotting the soul out of the world?"

"How do you feel about Hurtado?" asked Seabold.

"Old Agosto? Great old fellow. If he had two good legs under him, he'd have conquered the world before this."

"Politics... They'll leave him to rot in the jungle, now, won't they?" asked Seabold.

"He'll have to go back to the sea and put what's left of his army on a boat," answered Easter. "The trouble with old Hurtado is that he's too stubborn. He fights bad luck like a bull. He plays the whole game on one number. Now, he's been shown over and over—the Admiral and I showed him—that he couldn't find his luck in San Esteban. But he still keeps trying the game. If he wants a revolution, why doesn't he try another country?"

"He seems to like this one," said Seabold. "You think that may be the answer?"

"That may be the answer. It's a bad thing to be too emotional, Joseph. Damned bad! Easy to hurt the thing you love. Look at Hurtado. See what he's done to San Esteban!"

"I've been thinking about him a lot, this evening," said Seabold. "What would he need for that revolution of his?"

"One good general with two sound legs under him, and a good potful of hard cash. That's all," said Easter.

"And you out of the way?" asked Seabold.

"I don't flatter myself too much. Hurtado is a hard nut to crack... But I know most of his tricks."

"I've been wondering," said Seabold, "if Hurtado could ever be friendly to a man of my name, after all the harm that the Admiral did to him?"

"I don't know. It would be the devil on him to have to use your name. Why?"

"If I took my money and went to him, I mean."

"If you what?" asked Jack Easter, sitting up from the cushioned ease of his chair.

"If I got together all the money I could and went to Hurtado... Do you think that my cash would be enough for the revolution, supposing that I brought along a good general with a sound pair of legs under him?"

EASTER, HAVING stared, leaned gradually back again and lighted a cigarette. "It's a wonder to me," he said, "that they haven't put you in jail before this. Don Ricardo is getting careless."

"Not a bit," said Seabold. "He doesn't want to cause an international incident over outrages offered to foreign citizens."

General Easter puffed at his cigarette and said nothing.

"Besides," said Seabold, "I've proved to Don Ricardo Rodriguez that I'm no better than a fool and a coward... He had a million and a half pesos out of me this morning."

"Ah-h-h!" murmured Easter. His face was veiled by a leisurely exhalation of the smoke. Then he explained: "You're a queer lad, Joseph. I didn't know that you were this way."

"I've changed a little," said Seabold. "I've learned something out of five thousand dollars that I didn't lend."

"No; not that," snapped Easter. He stirred a little; his color grew a bit hotter.

"All right," said Seabold. "Not that, then."

"Fact is," said Easter, "that I'm a damned traitor for giving you advice in a time like this, but I've got to put you right. Here's Don Ricardo with as many as ten thousand well-armed men that he can call together at a moment's notice. And here's that clever devil Marigny with all the money in the world to back him. Don Ricardo can take his time, wait till Hurtado's army of rags and tatters and sore feet gets out of the jungle, and then sweep him off the face of the earth. Poor old Hurtado! This is the last revolution for him."

"But suppose that Hurtado had my money and a clever general to help him?"

"He couldn't win," said Easter. "The cards are stacked against him. This grinning ape, this catfish, this Don Ricardo, is not just the man everybody would choose to serve, but the point is that Hurtado's helpless against Ricardo Rodriguez and the Universal Fruit Company, with Marigny's brains to manage everything. Think of what that Marigny has done, just now! To start a revolution just to build up the hand that he can lay to put the revolution *down!*"

"It's a smart thing to have done," said Seabold. "You wouldn't find much more cleverness than that even in hell."

"No," agreed the general. "No, you wouldn't."

He became thoughtful, picked up his glass suddenly, and drank it off. He continued to spin it between thumb and forefinger. He blew it full of smoke and let the mist curl out again.

"Well?" he asked, almost angrily, recovering from his thoughts.

"I was simply thinking," said Seabold.

"Thinking, and smiling... I don't like that. What's up your sleeve, Joseph?"

"The general who can beat Ricardo and the Universal Fruit Company. The general who can save the hide of Hurtado."

"You have the man in mind?" frowned Easter. "Why the devil are you telling me all of this? Look here, Joseph, we're enemies; we're on opposite sides of the fence."

"No," said Seabold.

"No? Did you say 'no?'"

"I tell you, I've found the right man," said Seabold.

"Tom Lennox—the liquor has him. A brave devil and a good brain for fighting, but the rum is in his head and bones. It won't come out again."

"Try again," suggested Seabold.

"Ramirez. Oh, that's a man. I almost forgot Ramirez. But no. He has too soft a place in Guatemala... That Swede of a Petersen? No, Petersen's in jail in China... Roscommon, dead last year... Mulford; I don't know where Mulford is. Terry Mulford is the man you have in mind!"

"I've a better man than Mulford," said Seabold.

"THERE IS no better man," exclaimed Easter, leaping up from his chair in one of those extraordinary bursts of activity that were characteristic of him. "Better man than Terry Mulford? I remember when the old *Marguerita* was lying under the guns of the fort, the rudder knocked off her, hell right under our noses, and every minute a shell apt to smash into her and hit in among the ammunition that crowded her from head to heel... God of my life, that was a moment for you! The tide holding us steady for the fort, drifting us right in at 'em, and the shells hitting everywhere. Mulford gave me his idea. What a brain! What a brain! We fired up the boilers, got the men into the boats, started the old ship full steam ahead and let the tide direct her, and the last thing before leaving we set fire to her; and there our rotten little army lay on the backs of the rollers watching the old tub flame as she drove for the shore... What a brain, Joseph, eh? What a glorious head on that Irish pair of shoulders!"

"Brain?" said Seabold. "I don't see how you got out of the trouble."

"Of course you don't see," said Jack Easter. "But the point was that when the old hulk hit the foot of the bluff with the fort above it, the fire reached the magazines and she went off like a Roman candle. She spilled streams of fire up that cliff as though out of hoses. She put out the moon and stars. And part of those rivers of fire—d'you see?—were spilling down on the heads of the soldiers in the fort. That didn't matter. But the same flames were eating into the thatch and the palisades and the barracks, and, by heaven, the fort turned into a fountain of fireworks of its own accord! So all we had to do was to land our boats in peace and trudge up that cliff and take possession of the cinders. That gave us the high ground, and of course the town was ours in the morning. No; if poor old Hurtado wanted a good general, he couldn't find a better devil than Mulford."

"I think he could," said Seabold.

"You think so? Name him then, Joseph, and be damned!"

"He's well known in this part of the world."

"Is he? Name him, then. Out with it! Who the devil do you mean?"

"I mean Jack Easter," said Seabold.

"Ha!" said Easter. "You think—by heaven!"

"Hurtado's a patriot," said Seabold. "You've always fought for money. You'd like the change."

"Hurtado!" murmured Easter. "Why, he'd give me to a firing squad. Hurtado! He wouldn't believe his eyes! Hurtado and I?"

He stood erect, stiff, with his empty glass held up as though he were proposing a toast.

"There wouldn't be a chance," said Easter.

Seabold said nothing.

"And here I'll have it easy for life. State pension—everything a man could ask for..."

Seabold waited.

"What would you get out of it?" demanded Easter, suddenly looking down at him.

"Marigny and Don Ricardo. I'd get the pair of them for fish-food," said Seabold. "I don't care about anything else."

"I've got to think," said Easter through his teeth. "Damn this wine, there's no body to it. There's no life to it. Jose! Jose!"

"Señor?" cried the hurrying voice of Jose.

"You son of a toad, you frog-faced flyeater!" shouted Easter. "What do you mean leaving a gentleman alone with nothing but this belly-wash? Bring me rum. Rum, Jose!"

Here there was a rapid tapping on the door, which was pushed open at once. The manager of the hotel was bowing on the threshold.

"Ten thousand pardons, my general," he said, "but His Excellency the President has telephoned to beg me to inform you that he has great need to talk with you at once. May I say that you will come?"

"No," cried Easter. "Tell him that I'm in bed with the fever!"

"Exactly, señor. But may I tell him that you will come?"

"Ah—I suppose so," groaned Easter. "Jose! My boots again."

He added to Seabold; "I'll see you before long. Go home and wait."

PRESIDENT RODRIGUEZ was noted for the courtesy and the fine coffee which he gave to his guests. He and Marigny were having some of that coffee, together with little one-shaped glasses of old French cognac, when General Easter came into the room. They both stood up to greet him.

"This is too bad," said Easter. "The pair of you can get on much faster without me."

"Dear general," said the President of the Republic, "on the contrary, discussions go forward on a more solid basis when there are three to talk; because there is always a majority on one side or the other. Pray take that chair; it is the only one that fits your long legs. Will you have coffee with us, and brandy?"

"Rum," said Easter.

Rum, accordingly, was brought.

"The question is about the young heir of the Admiral," said the President. "If he is openly arrested, he may become an international affair."

"And that might be very awkward," said Marigny.

"Tell me, Marigny," said Easter. "Are you French, Italian, Spanish, English or American?"

Marigny turned his dark smile on the general. One rarely could tell whether amusement or thought made him pause in this manner.

He answered: "My country is the one I have the best reason to love."

"You're a diplomat," said Easter, and swallowed half a glass of rum as he spoke. "But what's the matter with young Seabold? He's as helpless as a new kitten. Why does he have to be bottled up?"

"My people are superstitious," said the President. "They have not the forgetful nature of you of the North. They remember great names, of saints and men."

"I've just been talking with Seabold," said the general. "All he wants is a safe way out of the country."

"If he is free to leave, he will be free to return," said Marigny.

"Why, the people despise him," answered the general.

"They despised him yesterday; they'll pity him tomorrow; and they'll love him the next day," suggested Marigny.

"The volatile and affectionate nature of my people..." said the President, smiling behind his glasses until his two eyes were reduced to mere glimmerings between the rolls of fat.

"Well, what?" asked Easter. "Roll him in a sack and throw him into the lake?"

"Murder will out," said Marigny. "And then trouble comes."

He smiled at them both, a particular smile for each.

"An arrest and the jail, then," suggested Easter.

"A common arrest," said Don Ricardo, "by rough-handed soldiers or the police... It causes talk. It has an air of cruelty."

"Then what?" asked Easter.

"If he were taken by someone who is known to have loved the Admiral..." suggested Marigny softly.

"It then becomes," interpolated the President, "an act necessary though painful. For the good of the country, though our hearts bleed for the measure."

"Who would fill the bill for the job?" asked Easter.

"You, of course, are the only man," said Don Ricardo. He put his fat hands together and smiled over the tips of the fingers at the general.

Easter answered: "You two do the cooking and then I come along to clean up the dirty dishes. Is that it?"

"No, no, no!" cried the President. Marigny lighted a cigarette. Wherever he was present, time seemed of little object.

"You want to turn me into a sparrow hawk, to stoop at the small birds," said Easter.

"Come, come! We are three minds who are thinking of the good of San Esteban, are we not?" asked Don Ricardo.

"Between you and me," said Easter, "we're each looking for a soft spot. Marigny contributes some money; he gets several million dollars worth of cleared and cultivated rich land in return for his work. You get a good part of the cash he contributes for your own pocket. And I have a chance to be easy the rest of my days as soon as I've wiped out Hurtado. Why talk about the good of San Esteban? Will it be any better under the Universal Fruit than it was under the Seabold outfit?"

"The larger the organization, the more stable," said Don Ricardo. "In the hands of a poor young fellow like this new Seabold, what confidence could we invest in the future of the company? But Universal Fruit…"

He made his favorite gesture with both hands, suggesting infinite space.

"By the way, did you get a contribution out of Seabold before you cut his throat?" asked Easter.

"It would be a pity to throw away a source of supplies before it is drained," smirked the President. "I secured a small contribution, it is true."

MARIGNY LOOKED up, without his smile.

"Enough," said the President, "to retire some of the railroad bonds. Enough to help us a little through the present emergency."

"The poor halfwit of a Seabold says that it was a million and a half pesos," answered Easter.

"Did he name such a great sum?" murmured Don Ricardo. "But exaggeration is a family trait of the Seabolds."

Marigny continued to look for a moment at the President. Then he said: "If Seabold disappears, there will be too much talk. If he's allowed to go free, he can make trouble."

"The whole city knows that he's a weakling," said the general.

"Not weak, but nervous, very nervous," answered Marigny.

"What's the difference between weakness and the sort of nervousness you're speaking about?" asked Easter.

He filled his glass again with the raw spirits and sipped it. Don Ricardo shuddered as he watched.

"Cats are nervous, and they're dangerous when cornered," said Marigny. "I always keep an eye on nervous men, like young Seabold. If a pinch comes, they're apt to forget to be afraid."

"If you, my general," suggested the President, "were to go now to the house of Seabold, with twenty soldiers behind you, and make the arrest in the name of the Republic... You see that everything will be open and aboveboard. There will be no whispering afterward. The world will know that Señor Seabold has been openly and honorably detained by the Government."

"For what reason?" asked Easter.

"Why, to look into the question of certain back taxes which the Seabold Company failed to pay to San Esteban," said the President.

"Taxes!" muttered Easter. "I forgot about taxes! That's the tree on which any man can be hanged... I don't like this business, Marigny. The dirt of it would get even through gloves."

Don Ricardo said in a higher, sharper voice: "Either you arrest him, or we send the gendarmes."

"And Seabold is too big a name for a common arrest," said Marigny. "People remember the Admiral too well. He spent money like water on the poor of the town... A clever fellow, the Admiral—except that he forgot to keep on living."

"And you didn't make that mistake?" grunted the general.

"An error that all flesh is heir to," said Marigny, with his smile.

"I suppose it's up to me, then," nodded Easter.

"I knew that you'd see reason," said the President. "We hope that the young man will be reasonable."

"Reasonable?" echoed Easter.

"If he should be so nervous that he tried to escape..." said Marigny.

"Ah, is that it?" asked Easter.

"Well, observe for yourself," said Don Ricardo. "If the poor young man is arrested and becomes so highly nervous that he attempts to bolt—wouldn't it be natural for one of the soldiers to fire into him as he runs?"

"The proof is only that the bullet is through his back," stated Marigny.

"Ah, that's it, then. Taxes are the pretense for the arrest. And a bullet through the back is the final answer," nodded Easter. "You think that it has to be that way?"

Don Ricardo leaned forward to whisper: "Suppose the young fool joined Hurtado?... He has to die, General!"

"Well," said Easter, "I've shot rabbits before this. Good-bye till tomorrow."

SEABOLD RODE home under the dim tropical stars which faintly pricked their way through the continually rising land mist. He put up the mule in the stable, looked down the line of stalls at the lifted heads of the saddle animals, and went back into the big house. Robertson was there, writing busily in the library, with a stub-nosed automatic lying on the table before him. He

"You can buy yourself off. They'll shoot you dead and hang you up for the buzzards if you don't," said Easter.

"I'll see Don Ricardo in hell first," said Seabold.

made a move of the hand toward the gun when he was aware of Seabold. Afterward, he sat back in his chair to look the young man over carefully.

"So you've done it, have you?" asked little Robertson.

"Done what?" asked Seabold.

"Whatever you were after."

"Can you catch a train out of San Esteban City tonight?"

"There's one leaving in half an hour," answered Robertson. "But what were you—"

"Catch the train, will you?" asked Seabold. "You can do it if you hurry. On the way, drop a wire by code at the station. Wire to the head office in New York. Tell them to get money to Rio Negro on the jump. All the money they can get together. It ought to be a hundred thousand or so, even after the chunk that Don Ricardo jimmied out of me this morning. Then you pick up that money and come overland with it to Hurtado."

"Hurtado?" cried Robertson.

"You're going to tell me that Hurtado is the oldest enemy of the Seabolds. I don't need to hear that again, because I'm joining him."

"Join Hurtado?"

"You'll be late for that train. Will you start? Good-bye and good luck!"

"But Hurtado—"

"Good-bye!" called Seabold, and waved Carpenter Robertson out of the room.

HE RANGED through the rooms of the lower floor with a flashlight and an automatic to make sure that no soft-footed thief was already in the place; for the talk had been that the Seabold house would be looted by the mob, now that the face of the President of the Republic was turned against the company. He found the big chambers empty, with an air of waiting. He even went to some of the windows and flashed the cone from the electric torch over the paths and among the trees of the garden. The rain had been dried from the leaves long before this, but the rankness of the growth varnished the foliage with a new brightness. Nothing lurked outside, so far as he could tell, yet constantly he kept with him the sense that the house was besieged; or that the darkness was a rising water.

When he reached the kitchen and pantries, he remembered suddenly that his departure might take the form of flight and that he might need food. With that he made up a pack into which he put the necessities. For food he wrapped up some rice, bacon, coffee. Other matters he got from the second floor of the house, such as a good quantity of mosquito netting, field glasses, a miniature camera (he grinned at himself as he added this), an emergency surgical kit not too big to drop into a pocket, a shaving kit and toothbrush. This entire pack was very small and light. From the gunroom he got a 30-30 rifle, with ammunition for that gun and for the super-automatic pistol which he already was carrying. Afterward he made the pack snug in his room and got himself into waterproof clothes. Then he went down to the library, because he preferred sleeping out the rest of the night in that room to going up to the dankness of his bed with its ghostly breath of mosquito netting wavering above.

He pulled a book on Mexico from the shelves and settled into a chair with it. When he opened it, he found on the flyleaf; "From Porfirio Diaz to a great leader of brave men, Ronald Seabold, 1903."

That was thirty-three years before, with Diaz still entrenched in more power than any President of Mexico ever had held before or since; and that note from man to man meant a great deal more than the words conveyed.

He lowered the book into his lap and stared into the corners of the dim room, because he felt his blood rising, and something working in his throat which was happiness, or absurdly like happiness. There was strength in him also, and a certainty that he was capable of action that had not been in him before. It was from the moment when he had lost everything that he had felt that warm inward current begin to flow. A pack had been stripped from his back; and now perhaps he could lift his own weight and something in addition.

He passed into a dream of old Mexico, and the Admiral received in state by the President of the Republic, with guns booming and flags in the wind, and music, and cheering. That essence of glory was still stirring his blood when something wakened him like a dash of ice water across his breast. Footfalls were coming toward the front of the house, then spreading out to either side of the door.

Out on the *patio* he heard small jinglings of metal such as spurs would make; a door groaned open; people were coming down the halls, lightening their steps. A door slammed. The boom rolled through the house with many echoes, but Seabold remained quietly in his chair. He merely pulled it around a little so that a table was before him—a thing that would cover the automatic he held in his lap—because it was not proper that the heir of the Admiral should shout out challenges to people entering his house. It was better that he should be discovered in this manner, in the quiet dignity of the library.

The footfalls converged from two directions upon the door which opened upon the hallway. The electric light was not on there. The figures of the men were clothed with dingy shadow, with bits of metal sparkling out from crossed bandoleers, machete hilts, rifle barrels. Their hats were so big that it was wonderful that so many heads could pack together in such a small space.

Then a young officer stepped through the doorway, all bright and new. He unfurled himself like a flag, with the drawing of his big sword, but the thing that mattered was the automatic which was couched at his hip in the other hand.

"Señor Seabold!" he shouted. "I arrest you in the name of the Republic... Show me your empty hands, señor."

"Here, my lad," said the voice of General Easter from the background. "We don't need all that sword-waving. Stand aside, friends!"

The heart of Seabold enlarged with relief as he listened. Jack Easter came through the doorway in battered old campaign clothes. The holster at his right hip was rubbed to the yellow of the leather.

He said: "Seabold, stand up and show us a pair of empty hands, will you?"

Seabold rose slowly, because he had to slip his gun onto the seat of the chair. He made a gesture with his hands and nodded at Easter. The general, nodding his head over his shoulder, said: "I'll take care of this fellow; the house is yours, my lads. Fill your pockets!"

Then he kicked the door shut behind him and came across the room. A score of voices raised in the hallway a yell that spread like quicksilver through the entire mansion. The eyes of Seabold rolled to follow the noise.

"Stand out here," said Easter, "where I can see you."

SEABOLD OBEYED, rounding the comer of the table. The pale, bright eyes of the general flickered slowly over him.

"You've got something of the look," stated Easter. "The same damned scrawniness, anyway; but he was tough as leather when they tried to pull him apart... How tough are you, Joseph?"

"I don't know," said Seabold.

"The orders are an arrest," said the general, "and you're shot down when you try to escape... Ever hear that story before?"

"I've heard it before," nodded Seabold.

"There's one other thing you can do. Come safely with me to Don Ricardo. Promise him to raise every dollar you can find in the world and pour the stuff into his pockets. I'll see that he accepts the offer. You can buy yourself off, that way."

Seabold licked the dryness of his lips. He looked back to the chair where the automatic lay.

He shook his head.

"Don't be a damned fool," said the general. "I'm not fooling you. I'm telling you about your only chance. Don Ricardo's afraid that you might take your pocketbook to Hurtado."

"You told him about my idea?" asked Seabold.

"No matter what put the idea into his head, it's there. It's your life that I'm talking to you about, my lad."

"It's no good," said Seabold. "I won't do it."

"Don't stand there braying at me like a jackass and saying that you won't. They'll shoot you dead and hang you up for the buzzards if you don't. The buzzards begin at the eyes, Joseph. Do you come along with me?"

"I'll see Don Ricardo in hell first," said Seabold.

He kept looking from the pale, angry eyes of the general to the well-rubbed leather of the holster on his right hip.

"No brains at all, eh?" said the general. "Just a plain fool?"

"That's all," said Seabold.

Jack Easter sighed: "All right, then. I hoped you wouldn't be worth it; but that cur Marigny was right about his nervous men... How do we get out of here, the two of us? The Admiral used to have a canoe with a light outboard motor in it, down in the boat-house. Is it still there?"

"I don't know. What are you talking about—the two of us?"

Easter looked up toward the noise of dragging and wood-splin-tering that came from the room above them; other footfalls stamped and voices shouted through the farther reaches of the house.

"What have you got in that tarpaulin?" asked Easter.

"Some food—some ammunition—medicine kit."

"Then you *have* a drop of the Admiral in you," cried Easter. "And one dash of his blood is worth more to me than all the banana farms of San Esteban distilled into Paris and diamonds. Come on with me, Joseph... These dogs of mine, they'll be a while cracking the bone that I've thrown 'em before they're sure of all the marrow... *Hai,* I'm ten years younger! Through the window, *amigo.* It's only a step to the ground."

THE UPROAR from the house was far greater when they were outside than when they were enclosed by the turmoil. The yells, the crashings, the frantic bits of song rang from the attic to the cellar of the big house. The general paused to look back once toward the place, then he hurried down the patch toward the lake.

There were three sliding doors opening in front of three sets of ways that slid down into the water; each of the doors was heavily padlocked.

"The keys?" asked Easter.

"I've never seen them," said Seabold.

"You'll learn," said Easter. "When you start a fight, pick out the high ground."

After that bit of enigma, he smashed a padlock with a bullet from his automatic and they pushed the door open.

"Flashlight?" asked Easter.

"Here," said Seabold, and snapped it on. The light wavered to the right over a number of motorboats, big and small; and there was one fifty-foot cruiser that loomed like a yacht. But what Easter went toward was the narrow grace of a canoe with an outboard motor clamped to one end.

"There's a boat already down at the dock," said Seabold. "I was out in it this evening. A twenty-footer that will do fifteen knots or more."

"How can we portage it around the falls?" demanded Easter. "Take hold!"

They carried the canoe out to the edge of the water. When they sounded the gasoline tank, it was found empty. Seabold went back on the run, remembering the stacked yellow cans at the side of the boathouse. He was still within when he heard voices singing out from the house of the Admiral.

Easter said at the open door: "Quick, Joe! They've missed us! Paddle out. We'll pour in the gas when we're away. Are you a hand at paddling?"

"Never used one in my life," answered Seabold.

"How were you raised?" asked the general calmly. "Take the place in the bow. Step to the middle when you get in. A canoe is like a silly girl. Pretty, but needs handling. Steady!"

Footfalls were running down the path from the house. Somewhere in the background, rifle shots rang like sledge hammers on anvils. They were shooting at shadows perhaps. Splintered rays and waverings of light played through the trees from the pocket torches and skidded far out into the dimness of the lake. The canoe lurched forward with a long thrust, its nose dipping down under the weight of Seabold until Easter stepped in and righted it.

"Paddle softly; don't even let the blade drip!" ordered Easter.

Seabold worked obediently. He felt from behind the powerful, silent impulses of Easter. He got the rhythm and held to it; the canoe sliding lightly but stalling as in black tar at the end of every stroke.

Voices came bawling across the water. Lights spread like shining oil on the lake, flicked away, came again, steadied on the canoe.

"*Quien viva?*" shouted a challenging chorus.

"Damn them, they've found us!" said the general. "Make for the reeds, Joe!"

"*Quien viva?*" yelled the voices out of the thin distance.

Something skipped over the water past Seabold; the gun report, like a handclap, followed. Then humming insects sang in the air. The tall reeds, looking black and solid as the shore, were immediately before them when the voice of Easter bellowed suddenly: "Hurtado! Hurtado *viva! Viva* Hurtado!"

Then the papery rustling of the reeds closed around them.

"I'm a fool," explained Easter. "But why not tell them what they're hunting? It's a poor fox that won't show its brush when the hounds take after it."

Seabold was already working with hand and flashlight to draw the top plug from the gasoline tank; Easter held the opened tin and sent the stream gurgling into the tank. The little boat wavered in a steady rhythm from side to side, with the light from the torch sliding up and down the narrow fingers of the reeds.

They filled the small tank with a single can. Easter, taking the light, shone it ahead.

"We can push through to the open water," he said. "If we start up the propeller here, it'll foul in the reeds... Steady yourself, now; keep on your knees!"

THE REEDS gave holding to the paddle blades, so that the canoe moved rapidly ahead, and Seabold heard the general sing a snatch of a famous old Mexican song.

There the reeds parted, and with the same impulse they shot well out into the flat water. Something rattled out of the distance. That was the exhaust of a motorboat. Easter was spinning the starter with the cord, swearing a little, spinning it again. It coughed, exploded, began to roar; in a moment they were rushing through the black of the lake, putting out the faint stars with their bow wave. Easter called him back into the middle of the boat so that the prow might lift. The small waves spanked the bottom of the craft as the head of it raised, but their speed was greater.

"Listen to the thing roar!" said Easter. "Here we are running like the devil and telling them which way we go! Do you see 'em, Joe?"

They could not be seen; they could not even be heard on account of the uproar of the outboard motor. Something low and black snaked up at them from the right. They went by a little island, still gathering speed, and rounded the nose of it into a wind. Easter sang out to Seabold to get forward into the bow again to keep the nose of the boat down to lessen the resistance to the wind. They seemed to be going much more swiftly, with the craft on an even keel.

"Which way?" called back Seabold.

"For the cataract and portage it," yelled the general. "That's more than they can do with their lumberwagon..."

Seabold could hear the water already, at the lower end of the lake. It had a sound of wind through trees.

"*Ah hai!*" called the general. "They're coming, Joe!"

A small shadow detached itself from the blackness of the island

"I've a mind to slap him
down with a bullet,"
growled Easter.

which they had just left behind. Then the arching brightness of the bow waves was just visible as the motorboat headed straight for them.

"Are you anything with a rifle?" called Easter.

"No good."

"Hand it back to me. I may be able to give them a leak in the bows."

He kneeled in the sharp stem with the tiller between his legs. Sitting back on his heels he fired, snapped out the shell, fired again. Little lights winked on the motorboat; the brief, sharp wasp-sounds darted near the head of Seabold and he ducked to every one of them. When he glanced ahead, he saw the smooth lip of the water as it curled over into the first cataract.

"The falls, Easter!" he shouted.

"Lie down on your back," yelled Easter. "We've got to jump 'em!"

For the big motorboat swept up on them with a speed that tethered them in place, and if they landed, clearly they would have a storm of shot about them on the shore. Seabold lay down on his back, his elbows braced against the ribs of the canoe. The stars were steady over him. Then trees rushed past his face, the boat pitched its nose down into the sliding oil of a flume, and that windy roaring swallowed his senses.

The boat struck with a force that jounced the wind from his lungs. It leaped again, staggering, through a thousand small fountains. Even the stars were whirling back across the sky—and then out they raced on a rocking current that kept elbowing them, tossing them from beneath.

"Up!" shouted Easter. "Mind the rocks!"

Seabold had no chance to look behind, but his mind held a picture of a living monster behind them towering into the middle of the sky. His business lay before him, right and left, where little fringes of white told of the rocks; and sometimes by the starlight he could see the flat sleek of their backs. He had to reach for those teeth out of water, thrust against them, glance to the other side for the next danger—and all in a moment the canoe was slipping down a comparatively smooth waterway with thick, leaning masses of trees on each side.

The general was bellowing out a bit of an old Spanish song:

Your toe at my heel,
Your hand at my shoulder...

And then the roar of the cataract pinched away almost to nothing as they rounded a quick bend.

Easter shut off the motor and started paddling. Seabold followed suit, the water dripping from him.

"They go back," said Easter, half chanting the words. "They give the alarm. The good word is telegraphed to Rio Negro and all down the railroad. They send out their parties to cut us off... But there's as good a chance as a single number at roulette. What do you say to me, Joe? A man's a rat who won't play a single number now and then. And we've got a lucky boat under us. Did you feel her leap like a good horse at a fence? Joe, I'm a boy again; the world's our oyster and we'll eat it raw!"

THEY WENT down the river at half speed because the stream took unpredictable turns and twists; then the bellowing of a waterfall reached them over the crackling of the exhaust and they made a portage around it.

The portage meant shutting off the motor, wedging in through the snaky green arms of the jungle to the bank, and then hewing a way through the hothouse dampness and heat of the greenery to the bottom of the falls. That took an hour and a half, with Seabold bitten to a stinging rash by the mosquitoes before he was through. The only spoken words were terse orders from the general which he obeyed in silence. Up the slippery path which they had cut, they had to stumble back to the boat. At the first load they took the outboard motor and the kit. In the second load they carried the canoe itself. The reloading, the refixing of the motor occupied another hour, together with the portage itself.

Easter said, as he got into the canoe: "That cancels out our head start. Anywhere ahead of us, now, there may be head-hunters sent out from the railroad line on the other side of the river. Imagine whatever you please; it's likely to happen."

Seabold answered: "I'm a dead weight on you. I know that. I know what you've given up for the sake of getting me down the river, too."

"Whatever you know, don't be a damn fool about it," said Easter, and they were silent again as the motor shot them downstream.

Once Seabold said: "What of Mary Cosgrave? What share has she had?"

"She helped Marigny do his thinking," said the general. "That's a dangerous thing to do, but she did it."

"Does she belong to Marigny?" asked Seabold. "Is she his woman?"

"Ha!" cried the general. "I don't know. What do you think? If I had thought of that I wouldn't have... Why, Joe, could a girl like that sell herself to such a devil?"

"I don't know," said Seabold. "San Esteban—it does queer things to people."

"But she—well—I wish you hadn't put the thought in my mind! Let's never speak of her again. I thought she was something up there—up in the blue..."

"Maybe she is," said Seabold.

But Easter made no rejoinder.

The current was quenched in the stillness of a lake. Two or three lights sketched for them the black silhouette of a village on the left bank. They turned off the putter of the motor and paddled. All before them the dark of the lake was jewelled with shining rubies when Easter flashed the pocket light for a moment ahead, to judge the passage; those were the eyes of alligators, red as blood. And a man was singing on the shore near the village, hiccoughing with drunkenness from time to time.

As the paddles dipped and the canoe slid, Seabold asked: "What's the man singing?"

"It's as old as the Mayans, almost," said Easter. "It goes like this:

How many eyes in the forest?
How many feet in the jungle?
How many hands in the night?
How many voices, how many voices!
Stand close to my shoulder, brother.
In the jungle one man is nothing,
But two are better than a thousand.

It's a forest song, but the rivermen use it a good deal, also."

Quietly, Seabold rehearsed the words for they had a special meaning to him. Then the current took them once more into the winding anxieties of the river course. The motor drowned the noise of the mosquitoes. Only the burning of his skin and the shudder of his flesh told Seabold how he was being poisoned by the soft-winged millions of them.

THE DAWN came to show them for the first time, clearly, the brown streaming and boiling of the current and the green of the jungle showering down into it, with the lower ends of branches naked where the water had rotted away the leaves. They had left their clear sky. Now it was a grey ceiling with black thunderheads lifting above and through the luminous mist. After the green instant of dawn the full day was on them in a moment. The earth, the river, began to steam with the force of the invisible sun. Seabold looked down at his wrinkled clothes, stained with water and with sweat. When he glanced back at Easter he was amazed to see that veteran looking as bright as youth. He was busily unclamping the outboard motor, which he now threw into the river. For, as he explained, it was bad enough to be exposed to the eyes of watchers along the banks without carrying with them a drum that beat all to attention. The paddling would be much slower, but the silence of it was priceless.

"But there's never a soul on the banks," said Seabold, "unless we get to a village, and the barking of the dogs tells us a long time before we're close to them."

"You can't tell what this river will turn up for us," answered Easter. "You can't—"

"Quien viva? Quien viva?" yelled a voice. Seabold snatched out his automatic and looked earnestly about him.

"Up higher," said Easter. "Look up there into the top branches, and you'll see him."

The parrot was up there twisting his head from side to side as though unable to believe one eye unless the other would confirm what it saw.

"Bad luck! Damn bad luck!" said Easter. He stood up, the canoe trembling with his unbalanced weight. *"Ah hai, amigo!* Have you forgotten me? I am your young nephew, Jack Easter. Give me the good word, old boy."

"Quien viva? Quien viva?" insisted the parrot.

"I've got a mind to slap him down with a bullet!" growled Easter. But he yelled aloud: "Come on, old fellow. Give us a cheer. Go ahead and be the life of the party. Give us a *'viva'* for somebody, and stop that challenging."

The parrot slid off its branch and flapped up the river with its harsh voice yelling, *"Quien viva! Quien viva! Quien viva!"* until it was out of sight around the bend. And Seabold remained standing and staring after it as the canoe turned and drifted broadside.

"Bad luck! Rotten bad luck! Rotten bad!" Easter kept murmuring.

"The little beast wouldn't show us the way downstream. Notice that? Gone off to tell Don Ricardo exactly where the bloodhounds can find us... Well, what the devil luck have I ever had since the Admiral left the..."

Here he broke off and sat down to paddle. Seabold, falling to work with his sore hands, began to get sharp advice from the rear.

"Don't swing the whole weight of your body. The lower hand is only an oarlock. You lean against it with the upper arm and shoulder. It's the rhythm that takes the trick. Easy, easy does it!"

The sun broke through the mist above and turned the thunderheads into mountains of fire and dark smoke. The whole burden of heavy rain was concentrated in the black bellies of those clouds. Sunshine on the brown river turned it to gold, with cloud shadows following after. New cheer came to Seabold, as the river world stirred to life around him. They were rousing birds continually, great black ducks or little butterballs, or tall waders such as herons, cranes, egrets; and even a few hypocritically smiling flamingoes got clumsily into the air when the boat neared. Whole clouds of hummingbirds jewelled the air around a blossoming tree, and far up in the sky the sailing specks were buzzards, waiting.

Seabold lighted a cigarette. It was so damp that the paper kept burning back from the tobacco; a hot, slow smoke.

"What about your hands?" asked Easter. "Can they stand it?"

"They're all right," said Seabold.

"I can see the blood on the paddle handle," answered Easter. "A hero today is a dead weight tomorrow. Take it easy. You can keep on paddling, but don't try to lift the whole weight of the canoe by yourself. Easy does it, Joe!"

TOWARD THE midday, a waterfall, roaring, walked up on them. They found a rocky bank and climbed it with the canoe before the bole of a flood-water came around the bend. Somewhere in the hills a cloudburst must have fed the tributaries of the Rio Negro River; now the precursor of the main flood came down on them. Instead of a single central current, the river boiled and whirled from bank to bank. Logs, broken trees, drowning tangles of vines, swept with the stream; and sometimes a huge dark trunk came alive and lunged halfway from the water. Then the main head of the flood struck the long bend just above, and the trees that fringed the river went down in a long prodigy of noise. The force of the river redoubled beneath the bank. A large tree went by, rolling its branches under like a grotesque Ferris wheel, and at the top a big black ape sprang desperately from limb to limb on the treadmill. When it caught sight of the people on the bank, the poor brute stopped struggling for a moment and turned its head to stare at that island of safety.

It remained motionless on its branch as the tree turned and thrust it under the water. The poor beast did not rise to the surface again.

The bole of the flood now stormed around the upper bend.

It was not a sheer wall of water but a sloping mass all creamed over with foam, and carrying in its breast like a tumult of charging spears the naked tree trunk.

The noise of it was worse than the sight. It seemed to Seabold, as he looked up in the sky, that the clouds following the course of the stream were drawn by an enormous suction.

The river widened below the next bend, and the force of the flood was expended there with a wide roaring that regathered in the narrower stream beyond. The currents, more black than brown, rapidly sank toward normalcy.

Easter said: "Parrots are wise birds. Damn wise... We'll eat now, Joe."

So they cooked rice and coffee and had a siesta under the mosquito netting.

The hand of Easter shook Seabold awake much later. Voices

were chanting on the river. Through the shrubbery along the bank, Seabold looked down on a big dugout which had been hand-shaped out of a mahogany log, now speeding down the stream with a dozen half-naked Indians handling the twenty-foot poles that propelled her. In the centre of the boat five uniformed soldiers with rifles were watching the shores. The boat song and the boat slipped away from them in a moment.

"For us," said Easter. "What sort of a price has he tacked on our heads? Marigny would pay half a million, I think—and for ten pesos half of these fellows would cut a throat by night."

"Shall we try to make it overland?" asked Seabold.

"Let me have a look at your hands," said Easter.

"They're all right," said Seabold.

"Let me see 'em... Nice and raw, eh? If we can get down the river ten miles, we'll strike overland. But nearly every step of the way will be machete work, unless we have some luck and hit on game trails... Here comes another outfit looking for Uncle Jack Easter."

Half a dozen natives poling the dugout this time, and a similar squad of five soldiers in the centre of the craft, carefully on the lookout.

"Patient as cats, aren't they?" murmured Easter. "They have their virtues, these people... You know a jaguar will wait for a whole day on a branch over a game trail, hoping for dinner. And there are a hundred thousand pretty fair marksmen thinking about us with their mouths watering... We'll wait till twilight and then feel our way along in the dark."

THEY DID not, in fact, wait for the night, but when the sun had dropped into the west and stuck on the black spike of a mountaintop, they walked the canoe down to the river's edge and got in with their kit. With the first paddle stroke the raw blisters that covered the hands of Seabold cracked open to the red, and the cloud of his mosquitoes blew back like a veil behind his head, but the fear that lay before him was an anaesthetic against all pain. He and Easter peered around the first bend, found open water, and shot the canoe forward. The sun dropped; the twilight brushed across their eyes like a hand; the night came and the night noises. Birds of darkness had begun their chirping insistently, night monkeys were squeaking, the lizards kept up an undersong with their constant yep-yep-yepping, and then the booming call of a swamp bird made everything else small by the comparison.

They went down the river with the walking thrust of the paddles, the light run of the canoe in between. Sometimes only the eye or the instinct of Easter found the way; sometimes the clouds gave back and the starlight touched the river from shore to shore. They passed a shelving bank. A vast thing slid from it, the water gurgling as it sank, and Seabold remembered with disgust the ruby eyes of the alligators in the lake.

There was no talking, and now he was alone with the pain of his hands, the tropical heat that made breathing difficult, the long and rhythmical swaying of his body. He could not guess at the miles which had flowed out behind him when a light flickered from the deep, inset mouth of a tributary, then poured full and strong upon them. A machine gun ripped the night open like tearing sailcloth. The water dashed about them, bullets thumped rapidly against the high bank beside them.

"Shore!" cried Easter. A sweep of the paddles brought them to it.

Another light joined the first. Seabold saw Easter jump like a long-legged kangaroo up the bank. Bullets mowed down the tall, green herbage behind his feet. The gun ceased, and in the cessation Seabold himself jumped ashore with the rifle. The kit already had been taken by the general, and Seabold was light for his dash into shelter. The machine gun followed him. The air was alive with it; the bullets were flying fists against the thick tree trunks as he dived toward the voice of Easter into the protection of jutting rocks at the rim of the bank.

He could see the launch coming across the river now, big and black behind its headlights.

"Now if we can give them a taste..." said the general picking up the rifle.

He lay flat on his stomach.

"Eeny, meeny, minie, moe; catch a nigger by the toe..." said the general, and fired. A second shot and a third followed. The launch swerved away. Without haste, Jack Easter continued to fire into her. The machine gun was still, rattled, was still again. She was in full flight with the headlights gone, and one endlessly screaming voice of agony trailing behind her.

The general stopped shooting.

"Through the belly, I guess," he observed. "Sometimes they yell like that when they get it through the belly."

"Do we try to get down the river bank? The canoe's gone," said Seabold. "And that was good shooting, general!"

"There's no use getting down this side of the river. It's the other side that we want to reach," said Easter. "Yes, I seem to have touched them up a little. I kept trying just for that point under the lights—just under the lights."

He laughed, exultant.

"The canoe's gone. Do you think we can find somebody to ferry us across?" asked Seabold.

"Ferry? Ferry us to hell! We'll see about that. Now's the time to sleep."

"They'll come back to hunt for us," suggested Seabold.

"Not they," answered the general. "Not till they have daylight; and even then they'll feel their way as if it were dark... See 'em scoot down the river to pick up the canoe? That's enough for 'em. That's a scalp to boast about!"

He snarled beneath his breath.

"I can eat some raw bacon. Then we'll turn in," he said.

THEY DID as he directed. To the hunger of Seabold the raw bacon was not disgusting; and then they slept under the mosquito netting until Seabold wakened with one side of his body on fire.

The general already was on his feet, snapping: "Ants! The army ants, Joe!"

He floundered into a bit of standing water behind their camping ground.

"Get your clothes off and wash 'em away!" called Easter.

It was already the small beginning of the dawn as Seabold reached for his rifle with one hand and for his boots with the other. The leather was greasy with overnight mold. When he stepped on the ground, it was alive with little hurrying objects that bit the sole of his foot, that swarmed up over his toes, still biting; as though he had stepped into a powerful acid.

The dawn light was sluicing down through the ravines of mountainous clouds, as he ran with prancing steps into the pool of water to join the general. He sank to the knees in the wet and slime of the pond. Easter already was pulling off the clothes into which the ants had worked. Seabold followed suit and started brushing off the specks of fire.

All about them the night noises had hushed. There was only the sweep of the river with its continual sucking and bubbling sounds along the bank. In addition, from the ground, from the trees, came a distinct rustling and grinding as hundreds of millions of mandibles worked.

A toad leaped over the ground with shorter and shorter jumps. It paused, staggered, and turned into a furred ball. The fur had a wriggling life of its own. A snake came out of a hole racing, but slowed as though it were trying to worm forward through mud. It coiled, thrashing, and then gradually stretched out.

One big tree stood near the pool, advanced a few clear paces from the rest of the jungle. Out of its branches small, living things commenced to fall, struggled a few moments on the ground, and were still. Those were the lizards. Other small creatures ran to the lip of the water, shrank from the touch of it, and were covered by the swarming ants. Great spiders covered with fur, spiders with a leg stretch as large as the extended hand of a man, got to the rim of the pond and then stood up on their long legs and turned to fight. But it was as though the surface of the ground had grown alive. The myriads swarmed up over the great bloodsuckers and they collapsed, struggled a moment, and then melted away to delicate skeletons, mere glinting traceries of white in the moonshine.

Then something floundered in the upper branches of the tree. A horrible, human screaming began, and ended when a big thirty-pound monkey plunged through the boughs and struck the ground heavily. It lay stunned for a moment, but it roused with the frightful yelling again, stood up on its hind legs uncertainly, and worked with both hands desperately at its face. It began to hop away, yet had to stop and fight to clean its head again, always with that human yelling.

"Why doesn't it take to the water?" shouted Seabold, in a sweat of horror.

"They've eaten out its eyes—you see how it runs in a circle?" said the calm voice of Easter. "Give me that gun, Joe."

He took an automatic from Seabold, lifted it carelessly, and fired. The monkey collapsed.

"The screeching was a little annoying," explained the general, giving back the gun.

But Seabold stared with aching eyes at the big mound on the earth which was diminishing, melting gradually away. When he glanced forward toward the camp where the snake had lain, there appeared now only a single dotted line of white, the vertebrae.

"They tell a pretty story in Tegucigalpa," said the general. "Did you hear it, Joe? I mean about the man who'd broken both legs in a fall? They stretched him out in a hammock one morning and went off hunting. When they came back at noon they found the splints, the bandages, the clothes, and the bones; but the rest of the man was gone. The ants had been there in the meantime."

Seabold groaned faintly.

That half-human screeching began again from a tree on the lower side of the clearing; it was followed by the swishing of branches that diminished into the distance. The howling died down.

"That monkey got away," said Easter. "The other one's been turned into rations for a couple of gallons of ants..."

Something slithered out of the brush into the open, a little lithe ribbon of a snake that whipped itself along as fast as a running dog. Even that speed slowed, clogged; presently the tormented tiling was a twisting, clotted lump that finally straightened.

"That's about the last bugle call," suggested the general. "Those busy boys ought to be starting home now."

A moment later they splashed from the pool and kicked the mud from their feet.

"No ticks, no spiders, no snakes, no scorpions, no fleas... it's like walking on sacred ground, almost, isn't it, Joe?" asked the general.

Seabold, turning from him, looked back at the little white skeleton of the monkey beneath the big tree.

"Pretty loathsome, eh?" asked Easter.

Seabold looked at Easter curiously and said nothing, for the general's smiling was so genuine that he could swear that he had enjoyed this grisly little episode of the night.

"You see," said Easter, "that's what happens down here where the sun's too hot, and the rain's too heavy; the earth comes to life and eats you."

"Down here in San Esteban," said Seabold, "I don't suppose you could ever be wrong?"

Clouds already were gathering across the forehead of the morning. They could hear the rush and stamping of the approaching rain before the shadow of it reached them.

After one hearty downpouring, the rain became a steady drizzle.

"Watch the river," said the general, and went back into the jungle with his machete. "This rain will be sand in their eyes, anyway," he called to Seabold.

THERE WERE only the birds to watch, getting home to cavort among the upper branches, and the long-legged waders by the shore regardless of rain, standing with their heads cocked back on their long necks like javelins on slingropes. They stood minutes long, then struck; and even when Seabold was watching one of the gaunt birds fixedly, the speed of that whip snap always took him by surprise. Sometimes they caught good-sized game and tossed back their heads, and held their bills laughing open as they got the morsel down. Once in a while it was big enough to make them give a drum beat with their wings, afterward, to help the swallow down their throats. But it was good fishing for them all. The heart of Seabold hungered with envy as he watched them.

A motorboat went up the stream towing a pair of dugouts filled with riflemen who stared closely at the bank where Seabold and Easter had landed. The motorboat pulled so close in shore that for a moment Seabold gripped his rifle in anxious hands. But they sheared off again and went upstream, still very near to the bank.

The voice of Easter called to him a moment after that. The general was rolling down the sleeve of his right arm, panting, red with exercise.

"Forty men!" said Seabold. "They came up in a motorboat and two dugouts behind."

"I didn't hear your rifle," said Easter.

"Show ourselves to a mob like that?" asked Seabold.

"Oh, they know we landed here... Don't miss the good chances to practice, Joe. Ever kill a man?"

"No," said Seabold.

"Well, it's worth a try," answered Easter. "That crew will take no chances. They'll try to work their way down on us through the woods. But not even a monkey, Joe, can get through these woods without making a noise. So we'll have plenty of warning."

"What good will warning do us if forty men come on the run?" asked Seabold.

Easter ran thumb and forefinger down the blade of the machete and shrugged his shoulders.

"Give us a chance to thin out the weeds, that's all," he said. "Come back here and have a look. I'm making a boat."

On the ground back in the woods a big rubbery sheet was spread out. Seabold picked up the fifteen-foot mass and found it light.

"The rubber tree," said Easter, pointing, "and the bejuca loca—if one mixes the two juices, the sap curdles into good rubber almost at once. Strong, too. Try to tear it. Now if we make a frame with branches, we have a canoe."

The hands of Seabold helped Easter make the frame of branches and bind the branches with lengths of tough bark fibres, but the mind of Seabold all the while was harking back into the woods to detect the approach of man. Sometimes he heard crashing noises; but these were mere outbursts of rain that beat on the broad leaves as on drums. Easter shaped paddles out of palm stalks. Then they carried the rubber boat down to the shore. It looked like a canoe that had been broken in three places.

"Can you swim?" asked the general.

"Yes."

"Then forget that you can. If they come at us, keep on paddling for the far shore and let me try to hold them off with my rifle. We can't spend the rest of our lives playing tag with this damned river. We've got to get across."

They got across.

They saw only a single fisherman in a wretched dugout, patient of the rain, with his line dragged aslant by the current, and he gave them no more heed than if they had been a cloud in the sky.

They had beached their rubber canoe before thin voices shouted from the other side of the river, and when they looked back they saw riflemen on the high bank which they had just left. Some of them were brandishing their guns in a yelling rage. Others of a more practical mind were kneeling to take aim; but Seabold and Easter got into the jungle unharmed.

NEITHER JUNGLE nor mosquitoes had beginning or ending. Like chaos, they were and there was nought else. The only sky that General Easter and Joseph Seabold saw was a grayness that rained at them. Underfoot was no ground, but green slush. Overhead more green, dripping upon them, and yet no clean water to drink except the flat, tasteless distilled juice which they got from the round tubes of some climbing vines.

Now and then they found a game trail that helped them suddenly forward and made them feel free and strong. But presently it was sure to wander away from their direction; and there was a compass in the brain of the general that would not vary from the true north. He had estimated as well as he could the probable position of the army of the revolution; he held firmly to that estimate and aimed their journey accordingly.

On the third day they came to a village of three houses and one inhabitant. All the people had gone a fortnight before, and the jungle green was beginning to sprout up in the lane. In the last house of the three they found the sole inhabitant. He was an old man whom time had starved more than the lack of food. He sat cross-legged like an Indian on the naked floor of his hut, with no morsel of food about him. When he opened his mouth to speak to them, he looked like a death's head whose jaw never would close again.

"The army of the revolution," said Easter. "Where is it, father?"

"*Viva* Hurtado!" said the croaking old man. "He is there! He is there! Or at least a fortnight ago he was there, when the others left me."

Easter considered the direction of the pointing arm.

"Start the fire there," he said to Seabold. "Get some water boiling in the pot. We still have some bacon and rice... Why did they leave you, father?"

"The Panama disease came into the bananas. So they went away to find clean ground. They said they would come back for me, but I told them not to."

"They walked off and left you, father?" asked Easter, sitting down on his heels.

"There was no room on the mule," said he. "After the beds were piled on and the pot on top of all, it was more than the mule could carry. So they left me because I cannot walk very well. My knees go so—so! I still can rub out the wet corn for the tortillas and I can sew a little if somebody threads the needles for me, but I can't walk. The wits have gone out of my legs."

When the rice was cooked with the last of the bacon, Easter said: "This is for you, father. We are so young and strong that we can live on our fat until we reach the army. Then we'll send back for you."

He carried the pot and laid it on the floor beside the ancient man. But the peon shook his head.

"Now I am finished with the pain in the belly," he said, "and it will be easy to die... I sleep a great deal. I crawl over to that corner where the bed used to be, and I sleep there. When I wake up, I lie for a minute thinking that I am only a boy again and that the pot of frijoles is simmering by the fire and the bubbles bursting with fat along the brink of the jar. Then I feel my bare gums grind against one another and I know that I am old Pedro again, and here, and alone. So I crawl back here and sit and look out the door at that mahogany tree. It will not be very long, now. Sometimes I get dizzy and fall over, even while I sit here, so I know that it won't be long."

"Here, here!" commanded Easter. "Take some of this rice. Look! Good *jamon,* too. Good, fat *jamon!*"

"We've found 'em. Stand up, general!" cried Seabold. But Easter lay still.

"I have finished with eating," said old Pedro, "but a cigarette would comfort my soul. I finished the last tobacco a week ago."

THE GENERAL took out tobacco and papers and made a cigarette. When it was lighted, Pedro held up a skeleton, dirty arm, and blessed him.

"How fast does a soul mount, *amigo?*" asked Pedro. "Will it be swiftly, the way a buzzard rises, or slowly, like this smoke?"

"It will be the way you want it to rise," said Easter.

"Then slowly, slowly," said the old man. "Because I want to see everything for the last time. I want to see the river, and perhaps I can look down to the next village. Do you think I shall be able to look as far as the sea?"

"You will," said Easter. "You shall be able to see that far."

"It will be bright, will it not?" asked Pedro, earnestly.

"It will be all polished with the sun of heaven, father," said Easter.

"So! So!" said Pedro. "I never have been to the sea, and that is the only hunger that remains in me, except the hunger for heaven. Yes, yes, God forgive me, except the hunger for heaven..."

"Will God forgive you, Pedro, if you refuse the food that would keep life in you?" asked Easter. "Mind you, father. When we reach the army we send back men to bring you in a mule litter. Will God love you if you refuse help?"

Pedro held up a rosary of wooden beads and laughed a little, his voice shaking crazily away to nothing.

"Why, God has been my friend for these many years," said Pedro. "He has been my friend since the dog died."

"How did that come about?" asked Easter.

"I had an old dog that died," said Pedro, "and he left behind him a strong young son that was just learning to fetch and carry. The night the old dog died I stood outside the door of my house and said: 'God, I praise Thee, for You take the useless and leave the strong. That should be the way of a kind and wise God!' And the next morning I saw the young dog lying curled in a heap, with his upper lip twitched back from his teeth as though he were chewing a good fat bone. And he was dead. So I went outside my house that evening, which is the time when God is nearest the earth, and I said: 'God, I understand. Let there be peace between us. I, also, am old.' From that time forward, there has been an understanding between us. And He will forgive me if I refuse life and take death."

"Shall I force some of the rice down his throat?" asked Seabold.

The general answered him with a look.

"What would a priest say about this?" asked Easter.

"Priests and very old men are very much alike," said Pedro. "Or else they *should* be alike."

"I think we can manage to carry you between us," observed the general thoughtfully.

"A plant cannot live without its roots," said Pedro, "and how could I live without the look of these four walls, and places in the floor that were dug out in ways I remember, or the face of the big mahogany tree, there? In all of these things I am rooted."

"You shall stay here, then," said Easter.

"Thank you, my general!" said Pedro.

"Ah—do you know me, Pedro?" exclaimed Easter.

"I never have been to the sea, but once I was all the way to San Esteban City, and there I saw the great people ride in a procession on one day, and you were at the head of them all, beside the President, where the people were cheering the most."

"Why didn't you say you knew me, before this?" asked Easter.

"Because a great man without his greatness is a naked thing. Who am I to shame you, my general?" answered Pedro.

"True!" said Easter, startled to his feet. "True! True! It's better to die than to sink into the gutter."

"Brother, it is best of all to know God," said Pedro. "One day you also may have a dog that you love, and the dog may die."

"We must go, Joe," said the general. "Take the pot along with you and we'll eat in the open."

"And leave him?" asked Seabold.

"Leave him? Man, can't you see that he's not alone?"

So they went out into the open to eat the rice and bacon, and the old man blessed them as they passed through his door.

"He knew me!" muttered Easter. "He knew me!"

And he ran his eye gradually up the trunk of a great tree and rested his glance for a long time in the topmost branches.

It seemed to Seabold that between Easter and the old man there was a country which was still undiscovered for him, and he insisted no longer about Pedro. He merely said: "But to leave him here unburied?"

"The jungle covers its people," said Easter. "It buries them as well as a priest and a grave digger... Talk about something else, Joe. I've got a chill in my bones, and no fever to follow it!"

THEY STRUCK thicker jungle than ever. It was a dense green wall, a pale green like the belly of a lizard, and the machete could be fleshed in it from the hilt to the point. They slashed above and below, a high stroke and a low stroke, and pulled the tangled mass back and trampled it underfoot.

It was work in a steam bath. They were drenched with sweat and with continual dripping. Even the skin of their faces began to grow pulpy, and every time they gripped the machete, spelling one another, they had to close the fingers one by one against the pain. It was like grasping the blade, not the handle.

They got through to a game trail. It carried them in almost the true direction for half a day, and then the jungle met them again, a little less stifling, but still a green horror through which they had to tunnel. All day they worked, and when the night came they sharpened the machete on a stone and went to sleep where they sat. They had had no food for a long time, the labor was terrible, and the only weight they would carry with them was that of the rifle.

Jack Easter had begun to grin as he worked. It was not a distortion of the face, but a stern smile. His accurate mind clocked off the hours of the day, and at the end of each hour they spelled one another with the machete. Many a time Seabold attempted to work longer than his shift, but the general always pulled him back and took his stance in front of the green wall.

They were four days from the village before Easter collapsed. He had taken a full stroke with the machete and then fell forward on his face.

Seabold turned him over. Half-open, glazed eyes looked up at him. He took the head of the general between his hands and shook it gently. His hands left marks of blood.

He shouted. The sound of his own voice was like an answer. Lonely terror got hold of him.

Then Easter's voice said calmly: "I've turned old and rotten, have I?"

He pushed himself up to a sitting posture and slouched his back against a tree trunk.

"You've been doing the work of three men!" cried Seabold. "What are you talking about?"

"Be still," said Easter.

Seabold looked down at the bowed head, the coat all rotted and torn, the shirt decaying beneath it, the trousers tattered at the knees and ankles.

He said no more but returned to the attack on the jungle wall. After a while, Easter stood up and took his turn until he staggered. Only then would he let Seabold take the machete away from him. When he mumbled a protest, Seabold pushed him back. His knees were no good, and he slumped to the ground.

Sometimes it seemed to Seabold that all the flesh was worn away from the palm of his hand and that he was clutching the machete grip with naked bones and nerves. His right arm grew inflamed. He had learned to shift the great knife to his left hand and labor nearly as effectively with this, but the skin and flesh of it seemed softer, more pulpy. It wore away.

On the fifth day, in the morning, Easter did not rise. He got no higher than his knees and then crumpled up.

Seabold worked alone that day, shifting the big knife rhythmically every twenty strokes from hand to hand. By noon, the general no longer could crawl forward to keep up with him. He had to go back from time to time, and carry the half-senseless body up to the place where he was working.

Then he stopped carrying. He picked up the weight by the armpits and dragged it forward, the heels on the ground, the feet wobbling back and forth. After each one of those journeys, Seabold had to drop on one knee until the dizziness melted out of his brain. The hunger pains ate into the middle of him. A dog was eating his heart out, a fox, like the Spartan lad. He pulled up his belt until it was biting him in two, like the belt around a beggar's monkey.

That fifth day had no ending. It had portions and sections, but no ending.

In one portion, after he had dragged the general forward a hundred feet to the cutting, in the tail of his eye he saw something wink and looked back to find Easter putting the muzzle of the rifle in his mouth and fumbling for the trigger. He kicked the rifle away. The front guard of it cut the mouth of Easter. He sat stupidly, touching the blood and then looking down at his hand.

Then he said: "D'you want me to be the death of two men instead of one, Joe?"

A horrible weakness came up out of the heart of Seabold and weakened his spirit. He began to sob. He said over and over: "Easter, don't do that! Don't do that!"

At last he could hear Easter answering: "All right. I won't do anything. All right, Joe."

A breathless soldier reported: "A foreign woman is in the house. She shoots through the doors. But one shell from the guns on the hills...."

Then he went back to the work. He felt that he had been unmanned, but in hell manliness doesn't count. Or does it?

A STAR shone in the eyes of Seabold. He was on his knees, because cutting a tunnel the height of a standing man was useless. But still he saw a star, with shattered rays, shining straight in his eyes. It was the twilight of that fifth day which had no ending. He was cutting by touch, not by sight; and here was a star before him, as though he were cutting upward toward the sky, and not straight ahead, on the ground. A soul, to be saved from the jungle, perhaps had to cut its way upward through the thick green...

And then the machete knifed forward through the tendrils into emptiness.

He thought he was entering a vast cave. When he blundered forward into the open, he saw that there *were* stars but they were above his head, and before him were fires, more golden than the sun, more beautiful than heaven, and dark figures moving about them, and the blessed scent of food.

He shouted.

"Quien viva?" yelled a man.

"Hurtado!" shouted Seabold.

"Si! Viva Hurtado!" shouted the soldier.

Seabold began to laugh.

He went back into the dark tunnel and stumbled over the body of Easter.

"We've found 'em... Stand up, general!" cried Seabold.

But Easter lay still.

He got hold of the body and draped the limpness of it over his shoulder. He felt as strong as a madman, except for a craziness in his knees, as he staggered out into the open again.

"Hurtado! Hurtado!" he kept shouting.

The fires grew bigger before his eyes. Hands laid hold of him, but he could not see the faces.

THE BRAIN of Seabold was numbed. As a drunkard clings with insane stubbornness to his limited ideas, fixing upon each with an infuriating singleness of mind, so he set himself to ward off danger from Easter. During that last agony of starvation and labor there had been nothing in his thoughts except the dread of the jungle and the fear for Jack Easter; now through a dingy mist of exhaustion he continued to guard the general. Like the memory of a drunkard, afterward most of the moving picture was lost from his mind and there were only scattered frames, here and there, that came back to him vividly. Throughout, the brown faces, the dark hands were not to be trusted and all their ministrations were to be avoided. The strange logic that operated in Seabold's semiconsciousness was that first Jack Easter was to be resuscitated, and then the wiser brain of the general would be able to take care of them both.

So he could remember the next day how he had beaten off the hands that extended toward them out of the bodiless darkness that surrounded him, fire-lighted with unearthly, long splashes of golden brilliance. He could remember seeing the pallet at a fireside and stretching Easter's long body upon it, and how the head of Easter lay, turned to one side, the mouth open, the face swollen with mosquito poison, arms and legs lifelessly sprawling. He could remember how he had pressed his ear to the breast of that senseless body until the slow, faint tremor of the heart was perceptible; how he roused from that great discovery and reward to find that brown hands were lifting the head of Easter and putting food into the half-living mouth; how he fought those hands away with the dread of poison in his foggy mind, then tasted the soup, trusted it, and so set his teeth on his own terrible desire and fed it swallow by swallow to his friend; how many men stood about silently and watched; how Easter first opened his eyes and how the swollen lips murmured, "All right, *amigo!*" and then how this speech seemed to release him from the long damnation of effort, so that he could lie down and sleep, sleep, sleep, his spirit descending through whirling darkness that might have carried him forever from this queer little world, except that with one hand he gripped the tatters of the general's coat as he passed into unconsciousness.

When he wakened the next day Seabold was prone on a good hammock that swung under a low tent whose sides were rolled up to let the steaming jungle-breath pass through. He roused from a nightmare, shouting: "General! General! Where are you?"

"Here! Here! Here!" shouted the voice of Easter.

And he saw Jack Easter propped in a similar hammock close beside him, waving a hand, laughing, restored almost to the very semblance of that cheerful fellow who first had entered the dreadful jungle.

"Are you all right?" asked Seabold.

"I'm as fit as a fiddle," said Easter. "And you, old son?"

"I'm right; I'm all right."

"Here's General Hurtado."

Agosto Hurtado wore a plain khaki uniform with no insignia whatever upon it, and only the red neckerchief of a general around his throat. He had a brown, round, featureless puff of a face like any other peon, adorned with a very Nordic brush of mustache. When he smiled, the vast bushes of the mustache parted like ten spreading fingers. He was smiling now as he took the sore hand of young Seabold gently and said: "The Admiral was too strong for me; perhaps with you, I shall be too strong for the others."

Without waiting for an answer, Hurtado walked out from the tent and his savage voice bellowed for food: "Soup—tortillas—coffee—roast kid—chicken—pork—wine —food! Where are the cooks? My friends starve and my army lies asleep!"

There was a table in the tent. Seabold got himself into a chair in front of it. There was still no sense in his knees, for they wobbled like the legs of a new-born calf, but he managed to get to the table. He was so weak that it was hard even to keep his head erect, but he would not lie back in the hammock to eat the food that was brought to him. He could have eaten a roasted ox; but Hurtado stopped him when he had had only a little.

Then he smoked a cigarette and found himself staring at the general through the smoke and laughing insanely from time to time, until his head fell in sleep on his breast.

WHEN HE wakened again, Easter was up and about, though the steps he took were short; and Seabold also was a new man, though for days a wolf was couched inside the spring of his ribs and devoured him.

The army was moving slowly through the jungle, following the line of a small railway, narrow gauge, which had been torn up by the troops of President Don Ricardo Rodriguez. However, new rails were laid and the little engines rolled over them, dragging the long lines of freight cars laden with men, guns and provisions. They went so slowly the jungle already was springing up and closing the gap which had been drilled through the forest. A corps of men had to go in advance to clear the greenery away before the rails could be re-laid.

Right and left, the trains passed little banana farms and great plantations in all stages of growth, as they climbed gradually toward the mountains of the uplands. But still the jungle was a huge wall of stifling green that Seabold watched from the windows of a caboose as the train inched forward. He had tunnelled through the sweating green of that hell; the palms of his healing hands itched as he watched the huge front of the trees go crawling by, enormous trunks that blossomed toward the top, and tangling, sweeping curtains of lianas falling thirty yards to the ground; then swamps starred with white lilies and with great butterflies blowing across them like flowers in a happy wind; then forest again, cohune palms that have forgotten to evolve with the rest of creation, cotton trees, ceibas, and always the incredible festooning of air-plants, with orchids making points and moments of loveliness. Now a hardwood monster 200 feet high with a writhing, twisting trunk and branches, painted in green stripes with moss an inch thick; then ferns delicate as the lace of maiden hair, or big as a tree with trunks as thick as a man's arm; now fragrances never dreamed by the cold North and rainbows falling through the moist air; then wine palms, coral trees, hollow cecropias. Seabold, as he watched them walking past, closed his eyes from time to time and drew a breath through pinching nostrils. The face of it all was splendid and strange, but he knew what it was to dig through the green smother at the foot of all this glory.

It was four days after he joined the army that the whole tatter-

demalion crowd was marshalled in the mud of a banana plantation, while Hurtado mounted a platform that was erected in the
midst and bellowed at the top of his lungs as he embraced Joseph
Seabold before all his troops, belted his own sword around the
waist of the young man, snatched the neckerchief from around
his own throat and retied it for Seabold.

It was a brief but strenuous burst of oratory that preceded this
making of a general. Seabold, all unprepared, was thrust up onto
the platform, blinking and a little dizzy, and while he stood there
he heard a friend of San Esteban described—one who poured his
fortunes into the lap of the republic, who clove to her fortunes
through evil and through good, who had placed his hand and
his heart at the feet of San Esteban. Who was that man? He stood
before them. As a gift of great price, he had brought to them
the greatest of military geniuses. General Easter, *the* general.
And now command was given into the hands of Joseph Seabold
himself, and the proud title, Friend of the Republic!

The speech, the sword-giving, the yelling of the army, rein-
forced and inspired by rum that was distributed afterward,
cheered Seabold and dizzied him at the same time.

Afterward he said to Easter: "But suppose that Robertson
doesn't come up to us with money? What will happen then?"

"It doesn't matter—for a while," said Easter. "The whole army
knows that you're with us. Every time a soldier looks at you, it's
as good as a pay cheque in his pocket. Yes, and the hard cash
already counted out for him!"

Then Robertson arrived.

HE CAME UP on a little blond mule that wagged its ears in time
with its stepping. He had a bullet-hole through the flap of his coat
and ruinous news to tell Hurtado: The men of Don Ricardo had
broken through below and were masters of the railroad from the
heels of the army to the sea! No more provisions would come roll-

ing to them from the low countries. Nothing more would reach them from the sea. They had to get out of the jungle swiftly and fight out the duel with Don Ricardo's armies on the highlands above. Whatever the decision, it must be reached quickly.

When he had finished speaking, the little man lugged two sacks from his mule into the general's tent and poured out on the table 100 pounds of coined gold. It made a splendid heap. Some of the coins rolled onto the ground. Half a dozen of them were snatched up beyond the door of the tent by the guards who were placed there. Hurtado refused to take the money away from the lucky ones. He stood at the open flap of his tent and yelled to the rabble of his army: "You see what General Seabold brings to us? Oceans of gold, brothers! Money, money, my children, with which to fight for our country. A golden sword has the sharpest edge in every battle. Courage and be of great heart!"

When he turned back into the tent little Carpenter Robertson sat on a canvas stool mopping the sweat from his face and said to him, quietly, very quietly: "If ten thousand dollars will help you, there it is. But that's all we'll get out of the Seabold Company until Joseph Seabold himself goes home and unlocks the vaults of his bank!"

"Ah-h-h-h!" snorted Hurtado. "What is this thing you say to me? *He* must go? Before he returns, the revolution is mired in the mud and stilled in the jungle!"

Carpenter Robertson cast telegrams on the table. The code words were translated in a hasty pencilled scrawl. He gave them the abstracted information briefly: "Kelvin is elected president of the Seabold Company. He begs you to come back at once, Joseph. He tells me over the wire in seven different ways that, although you may own, personally, the greater part of the stock of the company, there are other interests to be considered."

He picked up a telegram and read off a portion:

Disastrous effect of Seabold's presence in San Esteban now undoubted. We are faced with total loss of all our possessions there. Hurtado's movements bound to die of weakness before long. Entreat and insist that Seabold return. We cannot furnish more money on top of the enormous drafts recently dispatched. Beg to suggest that older heads may have wiser suggestions to offer.

Kelvin.

James Princeton Easter let rum trickle slowly into a glass until it was full. He raised it to his lips and gave them a toast: "Here's to a quick retreat and a safe one, Agosto. Here's to a pleasant sea voyage afterward!"

Hurtado said nothing, but Seabold caught the wrist of the general before he could drink.

"Don't do that!" he said.

They looked to him for further speech, but he had nothing more to say for a moment.

Carpenter Robertson broke out: "What's that red rag doing around your neck, Joseph?"

Hurtado, stunned, was leaning helplessly against the centre pole of the tent at this moment. He turned his head slowly as Seabold answered: "It's a gift from General Hurtado. He gave me a sword to go along with it, Robertson, and I'm going to use it."

Carpenter Robertson said: "Oh, curse it, is it going to be as kindergarten as all this? Joseph, do I have to start at the beginning and argue? Don't you see that the only thing for you to do is to take your fine sword and go home?"

Seabold suddenly laughed. He took the glass of rum from the hand of Easter and shouted: *"Viva! Viva* the revolution! *Viva* Hurtado! *Viva* Easter! *Viva* everything! We'll march for San Esteban City while there's skin on our feet!"

And swallowed the rum at one gulp. The bushy mustaches of Hurtado spread their ten fingers wide apart. Easter began to slosh rum into the glasses, and Carpenter Robertson, stunned, allowed a glass to be thrust into his numb hand. All the other matters, the revolution, the fate of the Seabold Company, were as nothing compared with the knowledge that he had seen a drink taken unprotested from the hand of James Princeton Easter, as though by a peer, as though by a master.

TWO DAYS LATER they were out of nearly all sorts of food, particularly of posol. Posol is a sticky, pasty, white corn meal, cooked and soggy. The true Indian of San Esteban won't work unless he has his ration of it; and the moment posol disappeared from the provisions of the army of Hurtado, the Indian part of his forces was ready to go home.

They were almost on the fringe of the jungle when the three generals sat down with Carpenter Robertson and debated the future. They added Robertson to their councils because at every moment he saw the worst before them, and served as the skeleton at the feast.

Two days away lay the highlands, the end of the narrow gauge, and the army of Don Ricardo with General Tom Lennox at the head of it. Grim reports came back into the jungle, brought by scouts who declared that they had seen with their own eyes a very efficient field artillery which maneuvered behind strong, swift trucks; they had seen a whole corps of machine-gunners, and an army fat, happy, cheerful, confident, laughing at the ragamuffins who were to come out at them from the steam of the jungle. They had plenty of munitions of every sort, and the great Universal Fruit Company was pouring forth its hard cash in an endless stream. They even had built a small railroad line out from San Esteban City, a sort of improvised railroad which served them as the great arteries serve the body.

Carpenter Robertson brought a map to Seabold and pointed out the main features of their situation. The forces of the Government waited like a pair of strong jaws, ready to close upon the army of the revolution the moment it issued from the jungle. There was still time for Seabold to attempt to get back to the seacoast and thence home.

"Don Ricardo has more men, more money. What have you got to stake against all that?" asked Robertson.

"I've got Hurtado and Easter," said Seabold.

And that same day he was given his first important task to perform alone. He was to follow a narrow little branch of the railroad to a big banana farm on the right of the army. It had been the most inland of all the properties of the Seabold Company. He was to go there, surround the place by stealth, and harvest all the provisions which were stocked there for the use of the hundreds of laborers. He was to collect every scruple of food, particularly posol. At the supper table he talked things over with Hurtado and Easter; Robertson was there as a matter of course.

Easter said: "What will you do, Joe?"

"Why, I'll go there, surround the place, and bring home the bacon," grinned Seabold.

"You'll send scouts ahead, though?" suggested Easter. "You'll feel out your way? You'll remember that a whole army can be smashed to pieces if it's caught in one of these narrow trenches through the jungle? Then there's another thing. You know what to do when in doubt?"

"What's that?" asked Seabold.

"Let him find out for himself," said Hurtado.

"Find out or die, eh?" asked Easter. "Well, maybe that's the best way."

Robertson put in: "There's only one thing to do. You have four thousand men; Don Ricardo has twelve thousand. You can't win, Hurtado! But the right thing is to withdraw. Appeal to our own Government. Point out that the company has been robbed. Get Joseph reinstated. When he's recouped his losses, then we can plan another revolution and finance it properly from the start."

"Not at all," said Easter. "Don't forget that the girl planned this with Marigny and Don Ricardo."

"What girl?" asked Robertson.

"Mary Cosgrave," said Easter. "Look at their setup, all built on her. If there's any protest Ricardo simply answers that he's doing justice, not confiscating. The Seabold Company dispossessed the Cosgrave Company, those long years ago. It took a long time for the Don Ricardo conscience to get worked up about the thing, but as soon as he realized how the Cosgrave outfit had been injured, he wanted to do them right. So he transferred all the *acuerdas* that set up the Seabold Company to the rightful owners, the Cosgraves! You see? All simple, all legal!"

Robertson broke out: "Where does that let in Marigny and the Universal Fruit?"

"Why," said Easter, "that's simple. If the Cosgrave Company chooses to let out part of its rights to another company that will finance the working of the properties—who can prevent that? Mary Cosgrave will get about half a million in good farms out of this business. The rest goes to Universal Fruit. But the whole legal emphasis is on the big-hearted way in which the Government is doing right by the Cosgrave outfit... I'm tired of talking. Pass me that bottle."

"You send Joseph alone today?" asked Robertson.

"No," grinned Easter. "You go along with him, Robertson!"

SEABOLD SET off that day with a map, 500 men, and a very great doubt. The map showed him the way to the banana farm and its village of huts; the 500 men were a scramble of rags, dirt and irresponsible good nature; the doubt concerned that thing which he should do whenever he was in doubt—a thing which every good commander in this part of the world should understand, it appeared, but which a man should find out for himself.

They had to cut their way through the new growth which had

sprung up across the narrow tracks of the railroad since the trains had stopped running with the coming of the revolution. Some of that new growth was twenty feet high. And the little bridges that crossed the watercourses had been broken down by the Government troops or by the employees of the Universal Fruit Company, which now possessed the banana farms. Seabold, Robertson, and a few other minor officers rode mules or little mountain horses near the head of the column, within sound of the swishing of the machetes that carved the way through the jungle. On the whole, it was as cheerful a detachment as one could wish to see. Those round, brown-faced soldiers chattered with Seabold most familiarly.

They would say: *"Hai,* señor, how does it feel in the stomach to be first marching to battle? Is it cold there?"

And they would rub their stomachs and howl with laughter; yet it never seemed to occur to them that they were incurring any particular addition of danger by being commanded by a novice. They joked at him, they taunted him from time to time, but always in the highest good nature.

One fellow reached up to him a corn husk filled with chili peppers packed in salt.

"Eat, my general!" he said. "It will warm your heart!"

All up and down the line, since it was noon, the Indians in the army were squatting, eating their rations and finishing off with those chilis packed in salt, picking at them like birds at seed.

"It will scald your throat out," said Robertson. "Don't be a fool, Joseph!"

But Seabold already was munching a pepper. The oily fire that sprang up from it sprayed across his palate and into his nose. He could not breathe. So he shouted: *"Viva* the revolution! Brother, I am on fire—with happiness!"

Tears poured down his face, but he kept on with the peppers, picking up liberal pinches of salt. The burning oil seemed to strike into the roots of his brain, into the balls of his eyes. The world swam before him. The tears flowed in a current. And yet at the same time there was a queer comfort to the inner man in this red-hot fodder.

The Indians, in an ecstasy, grouped closely around his mule. They stopped it. They held the bridle. They pointed to the wet face of their general and their sides shook with laughter.

The savage voice of Robertson cut in: "You see what you've done! You've made yourself a laughingstock forever!"

But Seabold kept on eating and laughing and crying out: "If we burn on earth, we will find it cool hereafter."

Literally, he finished the chilies in that corn husk. The Indians, staggered with mirth, offered him a flask of their wine. It was sour and stale, but it carried some of the conflagration out of his mouth and throat.

"*Viva* Seabold!" the soldiers were crying, yelling with laughter.

One of them shouted: "Do not kill me with laughing, my general! Let me die for you with bullets. *Viva! Viva!*"

They were all bellowing and cheering.

Robertson said: "A fine, quiet way to steal through the jungle and surprise the enemy, Joseph!"

"Look at 'em!" said Seabold. "They're happy, aren't they? The whole crew of them as happy as can be, I'd say. What does it matter if they laugh at me, if they'll keep on laughing when the shooting begins?"

BUT THERE was no laughing when the shooting began.

When the head of the column cut its way through to the banana farm they could see the little squat village of huts behind the superintendent's house, which stood up on stilts. For a quarter of a mile of the plantation had been levelled to the ground, to give the defenders a clear field for fire and prevent the army of the revolution from creeping up to close range for a charge. The only shelter was offered by obstacles which had been too hard for the workers to tear down. For the banana farm stood among the scattered ruins of the ancient city of La Merced. Many generations before, that site had been laid out as a capital for the country, with its dozen churches and its palaces for the rich of the land. But they found out that the rains were stronger than their handwork; fever cleared away the population; presently the place was left deserted. Still fragments of a wall stood up a little from the deep mud, or the strong arch of an old casement offered a frame for glimpses of the jungle, and just behind the overseer's house was a very considerable mound where the cathedral once had stood. One lofty section of the nave still remained, sustained by its flying buttresses. From that artificial hill came the worst news for the Hurtadistas as they deployed from the green mouth of the jungle. The crackling rifle fire from the village was not so bad. They could stand it, dodging behind humps and fragments of decaying masonry, even scooping rifle-pits in the mud of the cultivated land, and popping back their own bullets at the line of huts from which the storm was breaking; but now from the heaped ruins of the cathedral field guns began to open. With heavy shells they smashed down the shelters which the Hurtadistas had found. With a plunging fire of shrapnel they raked the edge of the jungle into which the greater part of Seabold's expedition had crawled for shelter.

Half a dozen of those three-inch, rapid-fire devils were working from the cathedral mound. Seabold, beside Carpenter Robertson, sat in the lee of the butt of some old bastion and watched the havoc around him. Not far from him, a shell tossed into the air a bit of ancient wall that was sheltering three revolutionists. Two of them appeared no more from beneath the down-showering wreckage; the third came running and dodging like a snipe through the mud to Seabold's own place of refuge. There he sat down in that same mud, leaned his rifle against his shoulder, and lighted a cigarette. A flying bit of shell or of stone wreckage had grazed his forehead and a steady trickle of blood ran down his face, but he was as steady as a stone.

"Hot, my general, eh?" he said. "But if the fools would put riflemen up there on the mound along with the big guns, it would soon be a great deal hotter!"

Seabold, venturing to look over his shelter, had three or four bullets instantly whistling about his ears. They came from the huts of the village; hardly a rifle shot was being fired from the cathedral mound.

"What is your name, friend?" he said to the wounded soldier.

"Juan Jose," said the man.

A shell thudded into the farther side of the bastion, exploded, and cast up a vast shower of mud. The three were dappled with sticky blackness.

"Juan Jose," said Seabold, "this is hotter even than chili peppers and salt."

The soldier laughed.

"Can you get back to the edge of the jungle?" asked Seabold. "If you can, pass the word that everyone is to work over to the left among the trees. Finish your cigarette and then go back to them."

"And what will you do out there, my general?" asked Juan Jose, as he dropped the butt of his smoke into the mud.

"I'm trying to hear the jokes they're making in the village," said Seabold. For as the riflemen kept up their fire from the safety of their huts, they could be heard laughing and cheering. And hardly a shell burst without bringing a cheer from the defenders.

Juan Jose was laughing as he got to his knees.

"*Adios,* my general," he said. "When you find out the joke, will you tell me?"

HE RAN suddenly from them toward the woods. Almost at the edge of the jungle, he stumbled and fell on his face.

"They've knocked him over," said Seabold. "Who the devil would suppose that these fellows could shoot so well?"

"Ay, there's the last of your messenger," said Robertson. "Shoot? They're so poor, down here, that they have to shoot straight because they can't afford to waste bullets."

"Look! He's up again!" cried Seabold. Juan Jose, getting to his feet, ran with a stagger into the green gloom of the forest.

Presently other forms could be seen, in vague glimpses, moving toward the left.

"According to what I've read of Central American fighting," said Seabold, "our fellows ought to be making tracks for the rear; but see 'em still obeying orders?"

"People believe what they like to believe," said Robertson. "Fifty per cent casualties in one day's row—I've seen that, down here."

He spoke from the side of his mouth as he lay on his belly and took aim around the corner of the bastion. His rifle exploded.

"High to the right," said Robertson through his teeth. "I'm always that kind of a fool!"

He fired again. *"Viva* the revolution! Joseph, this is something like."

He began to cackle like a hen; but Seabold was watching a group of four of his men running from an advanced post back toward the woods. One of them fell and did not rise; the other three gained that insecure shelter of the cloudy green of the trees.

"Stay here," said Seabold, patting the hip of Robertson. "See if you can snag another one of 'em."

He stood up. It was like rising, naked, into a cold wind.

"Amigos! Companeros!" he shouted to the scattered ruins that lay between him and the jungle. "Come on with me for the guns! We charge, brothers!"

Here invisible fingers plucked his hat to the side of his head. He heard the wasp sound of the bullet go by. But up from the scattered ruins jumped single men and small groups; and another swarm poured out from the edge of the jungle just in front of the cathedral hill.

They were yelling "Charge!" or *"Viva!"* It seemed to the excited brain of Seabold that they were standing still, jumping up and down, brandishing their rifles like fools who expected to frighten their enemies away from the field.

Then he saw little Carpenter Robertson go by him like a weazened old jackrabbit, bent low, swing his rifle so that it almost dragged in the mud. He was heading straight for the cathedral guns.

Seabold went past him, shouting: "Take cover, you old fool!"

He was too late. Robertson was down, hands clutching at his throat. One moment, a man in agony. The next, a still figure sprawled motionless in the mud. "He's dead." Instinct spoke in Seabold. Then: "They've killed him!" Cold fury possessed him.

Three shells in a single salvo struck the ground in front of him and threw up black volcanoes of earth. His men ran through the descending shower of mud. He could not keep up with them. A good leader ought to be that in fact. If only he had had sound footing to travel over...

A voice that was not his own, a bestial, yelling voice tore his throat. He could not tell what he was shouting. One small part of his soul, an aloof witness, watched him sliding and floundering through the mud. All he wanted was to find up there among the guns that dark face of Marigny and the fat smile of Don Ricardo.

The slope grew sharper. He fell over a stone and barked both shins.

He found that he was yelling: "Wait for me!... Smash 'em!... Down with 'em!... *Viva!*... Hurtado!"

And then he was up there among the guns, each in a neatly hollowed emplacement. A scattering of fugitives scampered down the farther side of the cathedral hill; other soldiers of the Government already were fleeing from the village as they saw the vital point of their line in the hands of the Hurtadistas. Some of his own men, shouting drunkenly, were pulling the guns around to turn them on the huts. But there was no time for that. He felt with a strange sort of agony that every fugitive who escaped was a priceless treasure that had slipped through his fingers.

He began to yell, "Charge! Charge!" And ran down the slope toward the village.

HE COULD see the little field of that battle as he ran. All firing from the huts had ended. Still, from the verge of the jungle, the more laggard part of his small army was streaming out. And again active, brown-skinned men sped past him while he damned the mud, the weight of his boots... If he could get his hands on one enemy; if he could drive one bullet through living flesh...

He carried a rifle like a club, with the butt forward, shouting: "Leave the street. Cut in behind the houses. Cut in behind!"

For there was that maddening wastage of fugitives who streaked away into the depths of the plantation. His men, running faster and faster before him, veered off at his direction behind the little town. He was staggering on through the mud with no one near him when a dozen armed men lurched out from the rear of a hut. There was such a madness on Seabold that he ran at them with his clubbed rifle raised. They shrank from him. They threw down their guns and fell on their knees. They lifted their empty hands into the air toward him and screamed out for mercy. It was seeing that picture that sobered him with a sudden stroke. He leaned on his rifle, gasping. Lungs and throat burned as though he had been running for an hour against the wind.

Twelve men, all on their knees, surrendering; and he alone with his rifle grasped like a truncheon. He had wanted to smash out their brains. He had felt that their brains would be paper under his blows. Now, abruptly, he saw that they had human faces. He was sick. He wanted to vomit.

More of his men poured about him. They were spreading through the village, smashing things.

"These are yours, my general," said one of his soldiers, pointing to the grovelling shapes. "What will you do with them?"

He got the answer somewhere out of a book.

"Send 'em to the rear," he said, and gladly turned his back on them.

He had to think about things, and his brain was not fit for thought. He wanted to sit down and recall that he had been a blind beast and try to get back to reasonable sense again; instead, he had to remember about getting the food supplies, all the food supplies out of the town. That was what Hurtado wanted. Then there were the guns, too, and the ammunition...

A breathless soldier was reporting something to him, making many gesticulations:

"Don't shout like a brainless monkey!" cried Seabold. "Now tell me what you want!"

"Yes, my general. A foreign woman here—in that house—she has barricaded the doors. She shoots rifle bullets through them. But one little shell from the guns on the hill..."

Seabold went to the hut. A score of his men stood back from it.

"Hello! Who's there?" he called.

"Are you a foreigner?" cried a thin voice from the house.

"Yes. Open the door before it's smashed open. Who are you?"

"Mary Cosgrave," she answered. "Will you keep them out? Will you keep their hands away from me?"

HIS SOLDIERS pressed at Joseph's back six deep as the door was unbarred from within. When it opened, a sudden pressure from behind flung Seabold into the room. The girl had slunk back into a comer. When the crowd spilled in at her she opened her mouth and made a screaming face, but not a sound came from her throat. Then Seabold saw that she had a big businesslike automatic jabbed into her breast. He turned around and began hitting brown faces with both fists. The men laughed. They begged him to stop hitting as they crowded back through the door, but they kept laughing like fools.

He kicked the door shut behind them. At once they began beating on it with their hands and shouting, *"Hai! Ah hai!* My general, are you leaving us forever? Come back, beloved!" and they still laughed like howling apes as they called to him.

He pulled the door open again.

"Will you be still?" he demanded.

"He is angry," said someone. "Forgive us, señor, and be happy!"

Instead of laughing, they were only panting, but the laughter was still marking and stretching their faces. He was able to hear other sounds beyond the happy shouting that spread around the village. There was an undertone of groaning from the near-by huts where wounded were lying, no doubt; and somewhere a man in agony screamed without cessation.

"Go to that fellow and do something for him!" he commanded.

"He has it here," said one of them, jabbing a thumb into his own stomach. "There is nothing to do."

"Go hold his hand, then. Fill him with rum!" commanded Seabold.

At this moment a handsome young blackguard called Colonel Moreno went by on a prancing little white stallion; another part of his spoils of war was the great scarf of yellow lace which he had tied around his hips.

"Moreno!" shouted Seabold.

Moreno turned his stallion and put spurs into it. He came like a charging bull at Seabold, threw the horse back on its hind quarters and skidded it to a halt. He gave Seabold a grinning salute.

"Yes, my general?"

"Have you been robbing a church, Moreno?"

"Yes, my general."

"Well, don't do it anymore. Get all the men together that aren't drunk and comb this place for every scrap of food you can find in it. There's the storehouse over yonder. Take care of what's inside it, and I'll have Hurtado make you a general unless you have your crazy head shot off before the next fight."

Moreno went off in an ecstasy, shouting orders, and Seabold turned back toward the girl. She had slumped down on a stool, the weight of her body falling loosely back against the wall. He stared around the hut to find a stimulant for her. It was a type of the Central American town house for the poor, walled with rough adobe bricks and roofed with heavy thatch. From the open fireplace in the centre of the floor smoke had crusted the rafters and the top portion of the thatch with shining black. The dried beef which hung from the cross-rafters was smoke-stained, also. The seed maize for the next planting hung beside the beef, the soot varnish guaranteed to keep off bugs. In the open corn crib in the corner, he could see the provisions for the year corded up like wood, also corn on the cob. Six people slept in the single room of this house. Ragged partitions separated the beds, which were wooden benches with supple branches spread across them for springs, and cheap palm mats spread over the branches. Beside the black of the fireplace stood the beanpot, the tortilla plate, a foot and a half wide, and the metate of porous stone on which the wet corn is rubbed to a paste. A few battered clothes dripped down from pegs in the wall. With these the habitation was complete, when he had found what he was searching for. That was a black bottle which he uncorked and savored the pungent sweetness of rum at once. He carried a dram of it to the girl.

She looked white and ugly. When the rum touched her lips she put up a hand of protest; her face twisted into old lines.

"Don't be silly. This will bring you around," said Seabold. "Take a swallow."

"Down to see the fun?" Seabold asked.

"This plantation is mine," Mary Cosgrove
replied. "And now it's ruined."

She took a swallow, fighting it down, shuddering afterward.
He, standing back to watch her, remembered the sleek beauty of
the girl in the black dinner gown at the President's palace. The

wrinkled coat that she wore now turned her into no more than a
pretty peasant. Her hair straggled in an unkempt tangle; a tarry
smudge stuck it to one side of her face. Last of all, he looked at

the heavy automatic, too big for her hand. He took the gun away and saw that the safety catch had not been turned off!

At once he felt ten years older. Nothing is so comforting as to be able to pity the strong, and as a rule her beauty gave her strength.

Here she began to rally, and he smiled when her first gesture was to smooth back the bedraggled hair. The looting of the village, which was going on full blast, furnished enough noise to cover the groaning of the wounded and to wall them in with privacy, as the noise in a French restaurant leaves every couple at ease and alone. Now and again men jerked the door open, saw Seabold and the girl, and went on, laughing.

"You came down to see the fun?" he asked her.

"It's all mine," she answered. "The whole thing—mine—and now it's ruined."

"This plantation—this is the only share they gave you?" he asked. "They have a big pie to cut up. If you lose this, they'll hand you another slice."

"What will you do with me?" asked the girl.

"Whatever you want done."

She shook her head as she stared at him until her eyes fastened on the red neckerchief. "Does that mean Hurtado has made you a general?" she cried out.

"That's it," he nodded.

"But then Marigny will never be satisfied until you're dead. And you're only a boy! Why don't you go home? Why don't you go home?"

"Against Marigny we have Easter, you know."

"That poor, old, sodden traitor!"

"Oh, that's what he is?"

"You haven't been here long enough to know anything. You're only a baby. You can't see what happens."

"I'm finding out."

"You've got to go home. You've got to go! Who's in command?"

"Where?"

"Here. I supposed it was Easter. He's the only one who turns men into maniacs. But even Easter can't win in the long run. Marigny—he has everything. Fifteen thousand men. Artillery. You've got to go home. I don't want your murder on my hands!"

She was standing, gasping out her words hysterically. He took her by the hands and made her sit down again.

"Stop worrying about me," he told her. "We'll begin at yourself. What sort of a deal did you make with Marigny and Don Ricardo?... Here, take another swallow of this rum... Now what sort of a deal did you make with the two of them?"

She took a bit of the rum, and seemed to forget what he had said in her distaste for the liquor.

He went on: "You hand over to Marigny and Don Ricardo your claims on the banana lands. That gives them their legal pretext for dispossessing the Seabold Company. And they give you a split of the profits. Is that right?"

SHE BEGAN to stare at him.

"Well?" he asked. "Without you, their whole machine would break down, wouldn't it? They wouldn't have a case that would convince any outside government, would they?"

"Of course there's not a word of truth in all that," said the girl.

He began to walk up and down the floor, turning sharply around at each end of his pacing. After a time he said to her: "That's why you say the killing of me would be on your hands. Because you cooked up the deal with the pair of them. Perhaps you're the foundation of the entire scheme."

"I have a right to everything I get!" she cried.

"Your father stole a small thing down here. The Admiral stole it away from him and made it a big thing. But it's all been stealing, hasn't it? Why do you talk about rights?"

"Because there's a difference between honest merchants and pirates!" exclaimed Mary Cosgrave.

"Your the honest people; we're the pirates, are we?" said Seabold.

He turned his back on her and found a group of soldiers passing with their hands full of loot.

"Get half a dozen horses here," he commanded. "Horses or mules. Anything with saddles."

He closed the door and faced her.

"How did Marigny happen to let you come down here?" he asked.

"I only slipped down here for a day," she said. "What are you going to do?"

"Why didn't you get out when the fighting started?" he asked.

"How could I dream that those drunken, worthless Hurtadistas would dare to charge cannon?" she demanded.

"What would you be worth to Hurtado and Easter?" he asked. "What peg would Marigny and Don Ricardo have to hang their cause on without you?"

She closed her eyes and bowed her head a little.

He stared down at her without favor in his eye. And a moment later the horses had come. He mounted her on a capable-looking mule, and picked out an escort of six of his soldiers. He called for prisoners and took along four of them. They were neatly secured with a lariat which looped around their necks after the fashion of an African slave train. Colonel Moreno, in the meantime, was mustering the long procession of men and beasts who were to drag back to the army that wealth of provisions, those lumbering three-inch guns, and the ammunition which was the most priceless treasure of all. He sent a messenger to his general to ask when the return march should begin.

"Start now," said Seabold, and took the way across the deep mud of the plantation until they hit the road that led from the village toward the plateau beyond. The going was easier, here. The exuberance of the jungle had been beaten down by the recent

Hurtado laughed till the
tears ran down his face.

heavy traffic and they made good time, until one of the soldiers
of the escort asked: "How far, my general?"

"I'll tell you when to stop," said Seabold.

They reached the green wall of the twilight, and passed through it
to the dark of the night and the feeble stars. He had not spoken to the
girl during the entire march, and she, slumped in the saddle until
she seemed no larger than a child, kept her eyes straight before her.

Sometimes the prisoners raised a moaning chant to help their
feet forward. Sometimes they walked with a heavy, despairing
rhythm. Again one of the escort complained in a hushed voice to
Seabold: "The news has come to the Government army; they may
have men on the march on this same road; we may meet them by
the thousands, my general."

"When thousands come, they make a noise, don't they?"
snapped Seabold.

They went on with the huge wall of the jungle diminishing. It
sank to a thick hedge; it thinned to scattering trees; they passed
over the gleam of the water on a small culvert and came into view
of widely scattering lights. That was where Seabold halted. He
set the prisoners free with his own hand from the rope that had
been chafing their throats.

Then he said to them: "If you take the lady safely back to Marigny or Don Ricardo or General Lennox, you'll have your pockets filled with money. Watch her the way you'd watch your eyes—and get on your way."

They drew a breath. They began to babble their gratitude all in a chorus, till he silenced them with a word. Then he rode over to the girl. There was only enough starlight to guess at her face, not to see it.

"When a girl tries to make a man of herself—that's where she's a fool," said Seabold. "A lot of men have died on account of you, today. Good-bye."

HE REMEMBERED afterward that as they waited in the darkness and watched the figures of the others draw away into the night, the girl had not said a word. At the time, that had not seemed to matter, because there was such an abiding anger in him that it filled up his mind more than conversation could have done. The freed prisoners, warned against speech, nevertheless could not help sending their murmured blessings toward him. So, at the slow pace of a mule's walk they advanced into the night toward the winking of the fires, and Seabold turned back into the jungle.

In spite of that excursion, he overtook the rearmost of the loot he had dispatched toward the central body of the army. It consisted of two of the guns, rather feebly manned with mules and horses and sinking into the mucky tracks which the other guns and wagons had made on the trail. He was glad of it because it gave him something to do. He dismounted and put his hands to the work. Two or three lanterns, each shrouded in a mist of mosquitoes, gave the light. They cut down shrubs and even small saplings, either to use as levers to pry the wheels out of the mud or as means of filling in the marshy ruts. All tempers were worn raw. The men cursed one another in screeching voices. Once a pair of machetes came flashing out in the dim light. Seabold fired a shot in the air and threatened to hang the men at the first sufficient tree. So they toiled right on through the night until a number of fresh draft animals and men, returning from the army, made the work light with many hands and hurried the two guns into camp.

It was not until he saw his hammock that Seabold was overcome with exhaustion. He fell in under the mosquito netting without so much as taking off hat and fell asleep face down, with the chorus of the night sounds diminishing to a dream in his ears.

When he wakened, the camp was lustily astir. A soldier sitting with true peon patience on his heels, stood up to announce that Generals Hurtado and Easter waited upon his convenience. So he went over to the one tent in the encampment, which was house and office to Hurtado and Easter. The moment he began to move, it seemed to him that the entire army gathered in his path; and every man was laughing. Men with little blue scraps of cotton cloth tied around their arms pushed through among their fellows to make the inside lining of the gauntlet through which he passed. These, bolder than the rest, pointed to him by hand and shouted taunts. They would yell: "Room for the little general! Give him more room! How can he pass?" And then the entire army howled with mirth.

One bold scoundrel snatched the hat from his head and went dancing before him, holding the battered felt on high and pointing to the two bullet holes in it.

"His brain is too hot, and he gives it air!" screeched the soldier, who was one of those with the blue bits of cotton around his arm. "Look at the nose with which his hat breathes! The little general— he thinks too much! *Ah hai!*"

At which the whole army again roared happily out of four thousand throats.

A man with a wounded arm in a sling was hoisted on the shoulders of two compatriots to see Seabold pass. He waved his free hand vigorously, shouting: *"Adios,* Don Ricardo! *Adios,* Marigny! Here is the little general coming! *Vamos!"*

This seemed the favorite jest of all. It was so excruciatingly funny that the army of the revolution fell to staggering with joyous laughter, and in the middle of this turmoil Seabold came to the tent.

When he strode in, Hurtado was laboriously writing out a paper with a pair of glasses that made him look like a bearded frog. Easter sat back with his heels on a table and nursed his usual glass of rum.

Hurtado pulled off the glasses and, looking up at his new general, said: "Hungry, *amigo?* Chilies and salt?... *Hai,* Juan! Chilies and salt for the señor."

"Stop all the nonsense!" exclaimed Seabold. "Frijoles, Juan. I'm hungry!"

"The little general says that he is hungry," said Juan, and then with his gravity completely overcome he burst into a yell of laughter and fled from the tent.

Seabold turned his bewildered eyes upon Easter, but the general was not a friend in need. He lolled comfortably, equipped with an immense grin that bulged a big wrinkle up against his monocle and threatened to push it from his face.

Outside the tent, Seabold could hear Juan yelling that the little general was hungry and called for chilies and salt, and this brought a fresh tumult of amusement from the army. Their laughter seemed to shake the tent like a wind.

"After the dance," said Hurtado, "I understand that you saw your lady home? Did you kiss her good night at her door, my general?"

AFTER THIS priceless jest, he opened the whiskered cavern of his mouth and bellowed with joy. James Princeton Easter was laughing also.

Seabold sat down on a stool which he tilted back against the centre pole of the tent and glowered about him. But Easter continued to laugh.

"Will you tell me what all this nonsense is about?" he asked Easter.

"He says this is all nonsense!" repeated Easter.

Hurtado, who had just finished laughing, began again until the tears ran down into the bristling hair on his face.

Seabold stood up.

"If I've made a fool of myself, tell me about it, general," he said.

"He wants to know how he's made a fool of himself!" translated Easter.

Hurtado, who was laughing as hard as he could, clasped his ribs with both arms to keep himself from dying for joy. Easter himself had to wipe his eyes.

"I'll go out and get some air," said Seabold.

"He says that he needs some air," echoed Easter, and Hurtado almost wriggled from his chair in a fresh convulsion.

Juan brought in a big, black-lipped pot of beans together with two corn husks filled with the infernal chilies and salt. And suddenly Seabold was hungry for them. He was so hungry that he forgot all the laughter and sat down with the big iron spoon that accompanied the beans. He began to eat, and into each spoonful he dropped one of those scalding chilies together with a pinch of the salt. At this, big Juan, the *mozo* of Hurtado himself, was newly overcome with insane mirth and ran staggering from the tent to give the news to the crowd outside.

"Oh, let them laugh and be damned!" said Seabold, and fixed his furious eye on Easter.

The general said: "Don't you understand, Joe?"

"No."

"He says that he doesn't understand," grinned Easter. But Hurtado could laugh no more loudly. He could only emit strange cries of pain.

"Tell me what you don't understand?" asked Easter.

"While you laugh at my questions?"

"Perhaps!"

"Who are the principal jackasses of the lot—the ones with the blue bands around their arms?"

"They are the heroes of the great battle of La Merced, Joe. Don't you recognize your own men?"

"And I made such a fool of myself that they still have to laugh? Is that it?"

"They had to do one thing or the other," answered Easter. "They either had to weep or laugh. Ever hear the old saying? 'What I love I tease!' Joe, the whole army is adoring you after that fight—and because you let the whole crowd of them rot while you took a girl safely out of the jungle! Can't you understand that? It was a good fight you made, Joe, and after all you found out the one thing to do in the pinch."

"What thing is that?" asked Seabold, scowling.

"Charge!" said Easter.

"Yes, charge!" said Hurtado, now able to refit his glasses upon his nose. "When we feel like running—when there is nothing to do—to charge. Always to charge!"

"General," said Seabold to Easter, "you're still pulling my leg. I know that it was only a little brawl. But it was hot enough to suit me."

"As hot as chilies and salt, Joe?"

"Will you stop laughing?"

He went on with the beans, but Easter only chuckled softly.

"So hot that you had to sit down in the middle of the shells and smoke a cigarette?"

"Well?" snarled Seabold. "I suppose that was wasting time. I know it was wasting time while the men were dropping. But I hadn't an idea in my head about what to do. I had to have a chance to think... Where's that Juan Jose? Is that man alive? I want to see him."

Easter walked to the door of the tent and shouted: "Juan Jose! General Seabold wants to see Juan Jose! Bring that man here."

All the mirth died out suddenly among the mob. Easter, coming back, put a hand on the shoulder of Seabold.

"Seem like a silly little whirl, Joe?" he asked.

"I know it wasn't anything," cried Seabold. "Have I *said* that it was?"

Here Easter stepped back from him and eyed him with a real concern.

"You'd better start saying that it was," he said. "Otherwise there are four hundred men who won't forgive you. They think they went through hell. Just a few moments of fire, and they had thirty dead and seventy wounded. That's twenty per cent in half an hour or so. Two hours of that and there wouldn't have been any army to laugh at you. Joe. Let those fellows know that you don't think they did some serious work, and they'll hate you and call you butcher the rest of your days."

SEABOLD, FORGETTING the beans and his hunger, stared.

"They think that they did a bright and manly job. They think that they had a brand-new hero as bright as a silver peso to lead 'em. But instead of kissing his feet, they choose to call him the little general, and talk about how he cried when he ate the chilies and salt... Then they tore up a blue cloth and tied it around their arms, as a badge for the victory of La Merced, and as a proof that they're your men for life and ready for all deeds of derring-do... Joe, scale down your eyes to a few facts. This isn't the World War. It's just a tidy little jungle scrap and La Merced was a fine job. Hurtado's writing out a proclamation about it now."

Here men came to the entrance of the tent. It was Colonel Moreno who entered with a brisk and soldierly salute.

"Hurtado, I told him you might make him a general," said Seabold.

Then he saw the red neckerchief which was already around the throat of Moreno and gagged on his last words.

"That Juan Jose—he is here," said Moreno.

Seabold went out from the tent and found, to his surprise, that Hurtado and the general in person were at his shoulders. A dense amphitheatre of soldiers extended before him, and at his feet, where the hammock and pallet had been laid on the ground, was that same Juan Jose of the day before. He could not be disguised by the bandage over one side of his face. His body was half naked, half swathed around with a voluminous bandage. Flies had gathered on the face and particularly around the one eye of Juan Jose that was exposed. Seabold dropped to a knee and brushed them away; and the crowd that watched him hummed like an innumerable multitude of bees.

"Juan Jose, I hoped it was through a leg that they pinked you when I saw you fall."

"No, my general," said Juan Jose. It seemed that in one eye there could be no expression; his was as bright and meaningless as the eye of a bird. "Zing!" said Juan. And he poked at his body with his thumb to show where the bullet had gone through.

"Is it much pain?" asked Seabold.

"I am at peace," said Juan Jose, and suddenly smiled. "Only..." he added.

"The man's dying, you fool!" whispered the general.

"What is it you wish?" asked Seabold.

"*Nada!*" said Juan Jose. "A cigarette, my general."

Easter passed one instantly to Seabold, who gave it to Juan Jose and held the match afterward. The army hummed again as though in anger.

"If you had not reached the trees," said Seabold. "If you had not carried the word—"

"Louder! Louder!" whispered the general. "Let 'em hear!"

Seabold raised his voice.

"If you had not reached the trees and carried the word to move to the left—they would have cut us down like weeds, Juan Jose. But the bullet couldn't stop you."

"You see," grinned Juan Jose, "it knocked me in the right direction."

"It was you," said Seabold, in the first public voice that he had ever used, "who showed me that there were few rifles with the three-inch guns. You showed me that the guns were as naked as babies. Except for you, we'd all be dying out there in the mud, and they'd be laughing as they watched us kick... Except for you..."

Here even the loudness of his voice was covered by a swelling, booming, guttural noise from the army. He was aware of a fringe of feet, a few shod, mostly naked, that had pressed very close to him. This wave of sound passed far away and there was a dead stillness.

"Except for you," said Seabold, "there'd be no victory."

He heard the whisper of a thousand indrawn breaths. Juan Jose closed his eye and smiled like a baby.

"I am content," he said. "I saw the charge. I knew, then, that I had a country."

Seabold brushed the settling flies from the man's face again. The last words were still echoing through his brain. He had been thinking of a certain grudge against Marigny and Don Ricardo; he had been thinking of banana plantations and of other trifles; and it shocked him to understand how much higher other men had been looking.

"Juan Jose, what can I do for you?" he asked.

"Señor, my general," said Juan Jose, "I am about to die..."

"You will live to be an old man and tell your grandchildren about La Merced," said Seabold.

"Señor," said Juan Jose, "in a dog's eyes that was dying I have seen what I feel in my own... *Hai,* the devils shot very straight, eh? Well, they also are men of San Esteban... There is nothing you can do for me, but I have a wife..."

"I shall take care of her," said Seabold.

"She's worth nothing; she's a bag of fat and talk," said Juan Jose, "but she's a good mare and she's bred well. I have also two boys by her. Señor?"

"They are my care, Juan Jose."

He heard a thousand indrawn breaths again.

"So—so..." sighed Juan Jose. "Perhaps they can learn to read and to write?"

"They shall be schooled, Juan Jose."

"So..." he breathed. "God bless you—and a little aguardiente if it could be found?"

Seabold lifted his head and held the bottle. He left that bottle in the hand of Juan Jose as the man was carried off.

Juan Jose was heard to say: "It is such a good, big bottle that it ought to last to the end."

Seabold, having risen to his feet, was aware of the thousand eyes fixed steadily and sternly upon him, but, perhaps because of the utter silence, he knew that anger was not in their hearts. He had returned to the tent before he heard the pattering of the bare feet as the crowd melted away.

THEY GOT out of the jungle into the highlands the next day. Half a mile from the verge of the lessening jungle they breathed the first scent of the evergreens. Some of the men fell on their knees and prayed. Others danced, their knees jerking up high because they were not accustomed to the feel of dry, clean ground under their shoes. To Seabold that advance into the open brought the most utter discouragement, for now he could see the entire army at a glance. Four thousand men were hardly a pencil stroke on that huge landscape of plateau and mountains, with the great volcano already smoking on the horizon whenever the mist cleared a little. Not only was the army tiny, but it was a wretched sight in the clothes which jungle moisture had rotted almost from their bodies. There were only enough rifles for one out of two of the men; they marched without order; they kept no time; they obeyed orders when they felt like it, as it were, and there was nothing formidable about them except the field pieces which raised a dust to the rear and the enormous swagger of the Hurtadistas.

Seabold was surrounded all day by men with blue rags tied around their arms. They still harried him with affectionate jesting; to one another they were like mischievous brothers; the victors of La Merced, in fact, had become a sort of fellowship, a club. It was not very much easier to progress over the highlands than through the jungle steam, for even a few days without rain had dried the surface of the ground and now a dust was flying, the heat intolerable.

Before evening they were close to a wide semicircle of hills that arched back on the left and the right as far as the verge of the jungle. Guns began to speak from the ridge of the hills. The Hurtadistas halted. A thousand cavalry deployed on their right. Another thousand moved down on the left. They came up fairly close in spite of the field guns and the rifles of the army of the revolution, and as they came little detachments made fake charges as though they would drive right down on the enemy, all yelling like Indians and swerving away at the last moment, so that only the dust they raised went billowing heavily forward on the wind into the faces of the Hurtadistas. There was a good deal of random rifle fire, but, so far as Seabold could see, not a single casualty on either side. He got to Easter, who sat his mule on a hillock in the middle of the plain.

"If they charged home, all those riders, what would happen to Hurtado's army?" he asked.

Easter pulled down his upper lip, took out his monocle, polished it, returned it with a similar squint to his eye.

"They would tear us up like a paper bag," he said.

"Besides those horsemen, they've got ten thousand troops up

there, and fifty guns, almost," said Seabold. "What the devil can we do against them?"

"I don't know," said Easter.

"But the plan! The plan!" cried Seabold. "I mean, what's the plan of campaign?"

"The plan is to march on toward the city of San Esteban, *amigo*, as far as we can go."

"Ay, but we're stopped now."

"So we are."

"Can we dodge around them?"

"I don't think so."

"What can we do?"

"I don't know," said Easter. "Look at that! There goes a real *bravo!*"

A single rider, detaching himself from one of the Government cavalry units, raced his horse straight at the Hurtado lines, firing a revolver as he came. He did no apparent execution, and, swerving away when he was only a few lengths from the lines, he shot away again toward the other troops. The whole army of Hurtado cheered this feat; there was no attempt to shoot him down; and out of the dusty distance the cavalry of Don Ricardo was yelling also.

"It's like a Buffalo Bill show," said Seabold.

"Yes," agreed Easter. "But it's free. Nobody has to pay to get in."

THE HURTADISTAS camped where a bit of a stream that wandered across the plain gave them water after the dusty march. The farther mountains, by this time, were smoked out of sight by a storm, and as General Moreno said: "We breathe dust today. We'll breathe mud tomorrow."

The dust had grown more burdensome every moment as the soldiers scooped out shallow trenches, outlining a long rectangle whose head was toward the hills and whose rear stretched back toward the jungle. Just before sundown, a rattling of guns in the rear persisted for some time. Then the report came up that the Government forces had cut in behind the army of the revolution, tightly boxing it up in the wide valley.

The quick evening came and went. The stars glittered more brightly than the jungle stars ever had shone. And minute guns began to fire from the hills that faced and flanked the Hurtadistas. That was bad enough, but other guns boomed from the rear also, and sent a thin whistling scream through the air. At regular intervals the firing continued; every four minutes, each wing of the enemy was heard from; but the calm with which the Hurtadistas endured was remarkable. When Seabold asked about it, Easter said: "These fellows don't care for what they can't see."

"In the morning," conjectured Seabold, "they'll blow us right out of this valley."

"They ought to," said Easter.

"Anything to stop them?"

"Not that I know of."

"Then, can't we retreat, general?" cried Seabold.

"Into that jungle, without supplies?" asked Easter, and Seabold stopped his questioning. He had come to the sudden realization that the army of Hurtado was strapped down on a guillotine, and that its head would be off on the morrow.

A group of lights came down from the hills shortly after night began. At the verge of the valley, it could be seen that a tent was being put up; then the lights went forward again. From the open flaps of Hurtado's tent, Seabold watched. Easter, prone in a hammock, was smoking cigarettes and blowing rings. Hurtado himself sat like a stone except when he used a thumb and forefinger to smooth back the incredible brush of his mustache. There had not been one word of advice asked for or given at that silent meeting, when the news came in that a flag of truce had arrived. The bearer was escorted straight to the general's tent. It turned out to be that tall Englishman, Jerry, all glistering in a fine new uniform. He had a trumpeter and a young lieutenant along with him. He saluted the three of them and let his eye and his smile linger on Seabold.

Then he said: "Well, gentlemen, you seem to be boxed up. But before the President nails the lid on the coffin, he's willing to talk with the three of you at that tent, back yonder. Shall I tell him that you'll come?"

"What will he talk about?" asked Easter, from his hammock.

"He has some bad news for a few of you and some good news for the rest," said the Englishman. "Shall I tell him that you'll come? There will be only three of us; only three of you. You see, the searchlights will cover the spot and prevent any treachery."

In fact, a battery of three strong lights from the nearer hills was fixed on the tent and made it shine like a little pyramid of marble.

"We'll come," said Hurtado. "Will you wear the bright uniform tomorrow, señor, in the shooting?"

"There won't be much shooting tomorrow," said Jerry. "Not at us."

He stopped as he was leaving the tent and turned, but instead of speaking his thought he laughed and went on into the night.

"Shouldn't he be blindfolded until he's outside the lines?" asked Seabold.

"This isn't a picture-book war," smiled Easter. "What can he see now that they haven't studied with their glasses from the hills? They know everything, Joe."

"Tell me, Jack," said Hurtado. "For what would Don Ricardo use such a man, and shine him up so much?"

"He gives the international touch," said Easter. "Don Ricardo respects the English. And Don Ricardo always manages to have a few of 'em fighting for him."

This speech reduced Hurtado to another trance, and Easter and Seabold were ready for the ride before the chief of the revolution moved. He prepared himself merely by putting on a hat. With his coat off, his shirt sleeves rolled to the elbows of his hairy arms, an automatic strapped to his hip, he swung onto the back of a mule. The right stirrup leather was shortened so that the end of his wooden leg fitted into the pouch prepared for it, and thus he jounced away in the lead, jolting up and down as the mule hit into its trot.

The army was already asleep, except for the thin line of sentinels which had been thrown out to all sides. Now that the gunfire from the hills had ceased, the valley was perfectly quiet. A patrol challenged them, and gave them a cheer as they passed on.

One of the soldiers called: "Papa Hurtado, bring me back a new machete, will you? The jungle has bitten the edge off mine all the way to the back of the knife."

"Use it for a spit, then; we'll have roasted Ricardistas tomorrow night," said Hurtado.

THEY SPLASHED through a shallow stream. As they climbed the farther slope, the saddle leather creaking against the pull of the cinches, Hurtado said: "Jack, how was it that we ever fought on different sides? We were brothers long ago, in the beginning."

"That was when we were both poor, Agosto," answered Easter. "You kept on being poor, and I turned lazy. And there you are."

"True," said Agosto. "I was as poor as a pig, and you were as lazy as a pig. There never was a man like you for knowing the truth and then doing nothing about it... Regard him, my little general. He has a brain; he has two hands; but his brain and his hands never work together unless he is fighting... Tell me, Jack, what shall we do?"

"We'll talk to Don Ricardo, and Lennox, and Marigny."

"Yes, I know that. But next to do?"

"Next to sleep, of course," said Easter.

Hurtado began to laugh and slap his wooden leg.

"Jack," he said, "what a comfort you are to my old heart!"

When they got to the verge of the lighted space, Don Ricardo himself came to the flap of the tent and waved to them.

"Come in peace, gentlemen," he said.

He backed up into the tent as they entered. Six canvas chairs had been placed in a circle. There was a centre table with two large buckets of ice. The long necks of Rhine wine bottles thrust up out of one of them; rum was cooling in the other.

Tom Lennox, as expected, was the third man. Both he and Don Ricardo wore khaki with the red neckerchiefs around their throats, but Marigny was immaculate in white linen. There was handshaking all around, a bustle of cordiality, except from Marigny, who stood in a corner behind his chair, and Seabold, who kept back by the entrance while his companions went cheerfully forward. Marigny, for all his dark reserve, shook hands with Hurtado and Easter.

"Ah, is that my Rudesheimer?" asked Easter. "Don Ricardo, you think of everything. I knew I'd be glad to see you, but how could I tell that I'd be as glad as this?"

They were sitting down before Don Ricardo said: "Ah, and the little general! We have heard a great deal about him in the last days... Welcome, Señor Seabold."

Seabold said: "Don't bother about me. I've simply come here to listen, not to talk."

"This is your chair, señor," insisted Ricardo Rodriguez.

"I'll stay on my feet, in case I should see a rat, or even smell one," said Seabold.

All five of them looked fixedly at him for an instant. Then Lennox said: "He doesn't understand. He's going to take this hard."

Lennox laughed; the smile of Don Ricardo froze deeply into his face; and the dark eyes of Marigny permanently excluded Seabold from all future thought.

"Well, Joe?" murmured the general, but after a glance over his shoulder at Seabold, he also no longer attempted to persuade.

Don Ricardo busily was doing the honors with the liquor. He served everyone except Seabold, who refused, and then Lennox proposed as a toast: "The good old days!"

"I'll go bottoms up, on that," said Easter.

That drink went down with comfort.

"Shall we come to the point, gentlemen?" asked Marigny.

"Let the point go for a while," answered Lennox. "You get the point too early and sometimes it's through the brain... Here's to you, Jack!"

"Don't be too personal, old fellow," said Easter, busying himself with his monocle. "Let's say, here's to rum."

They were drinking again, but Marigny only sipped his glass.

He said: "I'll wait on your time, gentlemen. But we only have one night, and a great deal to do during it."

"Here's to the night, then," said Lennox.

"You haven't come for nothing," said Hurtado. "So what can we give to you?"

"Nothing," answered Marigny's sharp, hard voice. "We'll have to do the giving, and it will be the odds... Four to one and the fox already in the bag. What odds do you call that, Hurtado?"

The old revolutionist grinned. "When you have the fox close to your hand, he's always nearest to biting, señor."

Don Ricardo laughed: "That's a good hit, Señor Marigny. You must admit, a good hit."

MARIGNY DARKLY admitted nothing.

"Now as a matter of fact," said Don Ricardo, spreading out both hands and moving them as though he were conducting an orchestra through an adagio: "As a matter of fact, when we stood up there on the hills this afternoon and watched you all walking into the trap like little fish into the mouth of a shark—when we saw that, we could not help laughing a little. I beg your pardon, General Easter. But the truth is that we laughed a little. And I said to Lennox, and he to me: Why should we make so much trouble for them? After all, we've known them a long time. We are old friends. So we decided that, with the agreement of Señor Marigny, we would try to meet you and find an amicable way out of the trouble."

Marigny, looking down at his glass, said nothing at all.

"Come on, amiability," said Easter to Rodriguez. "You have the face for this sort of a talk. Now what's the outcome of it in straight propositions?"

"Gentlemen," said Don Ricardo, "there is nothing we can do to show you our strength except to ask you to come with us inside our lines and see our troops and our heavy guns."

"Come inside your lines, señor?" asked Hurtado, smiling.

"We'll take you for granted, Don Ricardo," said Easter.

"I know you will. You find yourselves now almost four times outnumbered, in a bad position, cut off on all sides. We only need to wait in place. Soon you would be starved out. Or we can begin to shell you heavily from all sides. There is no danger that we'll run out of ammunition. We have a very good little narrow-gauge railroad that connects us with the supplies in the capital. You understand me?"

"It's a perfect picture," said Easter. "Go on. You have the nettle right in your hand. Why don't you close down on it?"

Here Marigny cut incisively into the talk, saying: "Blood does no good. People who walk in it will have a slip and a fall, one of these days."

Old Hurtado said: "You should know, señor. In Honduras, in Salvador, in Nicaragua, you have manured your ground with dead men. And I understand that bones keep the soil sweet for a long time."

"Gentlemen! Gentlemen!" said Don Ricardo, with his orchestral gesture. "Will you listen to quiet reason?"

"Go on and reason," answered Easter, but he smiled a little on Hurtado.

"What we propose, in short," said Don Ricardo, "is to permit your safe withdrawal, without a shot fired on either side."

When he had finished the sentence, he clapped both his hands together. Hurtado had started halfway from his chair, and then sank slowly back into it.

Don Ricardo went on with a sweep of eloquence: "What, gentlemen? We know one another. Agosto Hurtado, though we have differed in the way of it, we both have loved our country. There is room for us still to love it. The general for all these years has been to me as the glove to the hand. And as for this brave young man, it will be my special care, under a sacred oath, to see that he is safely returned to his own country, without harm. I will take him with me tonight and send him safely down to the sea; and may God witness that my intention is good!"

"That's white," said General Tom Lennox. "You let 'em off scot-free, Don Ricardo?"

"Free! Perfectly free! And an amnesty to every man in the revolution!"

Seabold said: "Everybody speaks except the devil himself."

Marigny had been looking down at his folded hands. He glanced sharply up toward Seabold and held him with a long look.

"We have agreed—all of us," said Marigny, and looked down to his hands again.

"What do you say, Agosto?" asked Easter of the one-legged man.

"I must think," said Hurtado.

"Think of this," said Seabold. "Think of the retreat through the jungle. Think of four thousand men cursing you for running without a fight."

"True!" cried Hurtado, his voice a groan. "But think of four thousand men kicking in the dust. Blood and dust make a dirty mixture, my general!"

"You keep young men about you, Hurtado," said Marigny, eyeing Seabold and then smiling sourly.

"The boys would die off like flies if we tried to take 'em back through the jungle," remarked Easter. "There's truth in what Seabold says."

"Why should they go back through the jungle?" asked Don Ricardo, once more exalted. "Why should they not disperse wherever they please? Let them fraternize with my own soldiers. There will be extra rations for them all. Let them go as they please, without the slightest pain... To have power is a glorious thing, Agosto; to use it mercifully is still more glorious."

Seabold said: "If you want to see how much mercy there is, look at Marigny's face. The shark in him is swallowing something this moment."

"My young friend," said Marigny, "it's hard to lose money as you've been losing it. But you've had a little dance, and now you pay the piper. Don't try to drag four thousand brave men down with you. Hurtado, don't forget that one fool can sink the biggest ship in the world."

HURTADO TURNED his big, round, peon's head suddenly about and stared at Seabold over his shoulder.

"You are wrong, Marigny," he answered. "He is my luck... General, what do you say to this?"

Easter said: "I don't really give a damn, Agosto. You decide as you please."

"If you fold up and run," said Seabold, "there's not enough water in the world to wash your reputations clean again. You'll sell rags in New Orleans, Hurtado; you'll die in a boarding-house back room, general."

"Come on, Jack," urged Lennox. "You don't listen to boys, do you?"

"When I was a boy," answered Easter, "I was a damned sight

more worth listening to than I am now… But go on, Don Ricardo. Tell us what we'll have to sign."

"I have everything here," said the President of the Republic. "For you, Agosto, merely a promise not to return again to San Esteban, and a few words to say that you believe the country is, after all, well governed… For you, general, merely the promise to return… And for the young man—why, nothing at all. Nothing at all!"

He smoothed the papers on the table more with his smile than with his hands.

"Well…" said Hurtado.

He got up suddenly, paused.

"You have four thousand boys out there in the dust," said Marigny, quietly.

"True!" groaned Hurtado. "True, true!"

He turned to Easter.

"Is it finished, Jack?" he asked.

"Not on my account," answered James Princeton Easter. "What do you say, Joe?"

"If they have us in their hands, if they're sure of us, they'll close in," said Seabold. "If they're bargaining like this, it means that they're afraid of something, doesn't it?"

"Of course it means that," answered Easter. "But Papa Hurtado is thinking about his four thousand boys… Agosto, don't sign on our account."

"Shall we—" began Hurtado.

Here a murmur that had begun out of the distance ran swiftly toward them, like the beating of a million small hoofs, and as Hurtado reached the middle of his sentence, rain crashed on the tent, driving through the canvas little sprays of chilly water that fell on the six men and their upturned faces. The alkaline odor of slaked dust filled the air.

Through this new uproar, the voice of Marigny cut as he said: "I guess this ends it, Hurtado. You were pretty helpless in the dust. You'll be anchored fast in the mud, now."

"Well," said Hurtado, "I've walked more miles through mud than I ever did over dry ground... Listen! By heaven, the rain sounds like drums! Is it a sign? Is it a sign, my friends?"

"Agosto," said Easter, "I knew that you'd never get to the signing of that surrender. The pen would have broken in your hand; and now the ink has turned into water."

He stood up.

Don Ricardo screeched out at the top of his voice: "Gentlemen! Gentlemen! You don't know what you're doing! We've offered you charity; we've offered you something for nothing!"

"See the pig sweat!" said Seabold.

That, so far as he was concerned, was the end of that conference. The spasm of Don Ricardo's anger after this insult, the sneering smile of Marigny as he stood aloof from the rest of the contention, Tom Lennox shouting out to Easter that the fight would simply be murder the next day, Easter's serious effort to finish a bottle of the Rhine wine, the rising bulldog in Hurtado—all of these things were afterward a jumbled memory. What was important was the ride back through the rain.

It came down so fast that the converged and overlapping circles of the searchlights were beaten into a twilight mistiness. One of those lights followed the three ineffectively for a short distance through the dimness and then wandered away.

The whole valley roared with rain. Currents of water sloshed around the hoofs of the mules and the horse. And before they reached the camp of their soldiers, they heard the dismayed yell of the army squealing through the darkness.

MANY LIGHTS were flickering through the darkness of the camp, like the silver threads of a spider's web, and the soldiers were as insects entangled and struggling in the trap. The minute guns of the Government forces began to speak regularly from the hills.

Then the heavens turned into one universal spout and the rain bucketed down, so that the tent of Hurtado, in which Easter, Hurtado and Seabold were wringing out their sopping clothes, sagged at the top; small waves ran through the canvas: the chilling spray forced itself through the weave of the strong cloth.

"Four thousand wet cats by the morning," said Easter.

"Good!" said Hurtado.

"Good?" echoed Easter.

"Good, Jack! Very good! Because cats will run to get out of the wet, won't they?"

"True! True!" cried Easter. "They'll even run at a dog to get out of the rain... If we drove them now straight back toward the jungle, could we cut through? I think we could. We'll get them under arms..."

"But the cannon in the mud?" suggested Seabold.

"Let 'em stay in the mud," answered Easter. "We're thinking about four thousand wet cats, aren't we?"

That was why the orders were sent out for the army of the revolution to fall in.

When the rain was at its heaviest, no other sound could be heard but its dashing. But when it eased a little, there was the squelching noise of thousands of feet in the mud.

Calls ran back from mouth to mouth as the companies rallied. Seabold, as the rain splattered on his cloak of piled silk, rallied his own contingent to the continued cry of "La Merced! La Merced!" And his men of the last battle came trooping up around him. When a pocket torch gleamed from time to time, it showed him faces streaming with wet but amazingly good-humored. They seemed to have no care in the world except to shelter their rifles.

Someone ran to Seabold with word that he was wanted at the general's tent. He waded back to headquarters. Both Hurtado and

Easter were there, newly come in from the rain, with the water still sluicing off their slickers. A boy as wet as a herring from the sea, with a rain-beaten felt hat dripping down to his shoulders and over his face, was confronting the two of them.

"Why?" Hurtado was asking.

"Because I saw at last that they were beasts—Don Ricardo and Marigny," said the voice of Mary Cosgrave.

"Wanted you to hear this," said Easter to Seabold.

The latter ranged himself at the side of the general and Hurtado. The girl failed to see him. She looked only at the other two. The rain had plastered her clothes to her body. Range women beside men, Seabold decided, and they're unimportant little things.

He got a blanket off the pallet in the tent and put it around her shoulders. Her hat dripped down onto the blanket. He took the hat off her head and wrung a gush of water out of it. Her hair, disturbed by this withdrawal of the hat, pulled all askew. It wasn't cut short, and it wasn't longer than her shoulder blades. She took that hair in her hands, tilted her head, and wrung out the water: then she twisted the hair around her head and made it stay in place.

All this time she was talking.

Easter had said: "Our boys pick you up when you're sneaking along our picket line. You wanted to distinguish yourself by bringing back some information. You wanted to play spy, didn't you?"

"There wasn't any need to play spy," she said. "Everybody on the other side knows that you're cooked geese."

"Oh, we're cooked, are we?" asked Easter.

"I had to escape from them. I had to get through the guard they had on me. Don't you understand?" she said.

"You escaped to us, and yet we're cooked geese?" asked Easter.

"Jack, we're wasting time," said Hurtado.

Seabold went back to the side of the other two. The girl's absent-minded glance followed him for an instant. She had expressed no gratitude. With one hand she held the rumpled hat. The other hand fastened the blanket in front of her.

HE KEPT watching her, half disgusted, half curious, seeing the truth of a good many things for the first time. If you see girls at a dance, on a tennis court, on the beach, you take them for granted. You're ashamed to look at them. They've been essential to other men and you feel that they may become essential to you. So you put up with them. Sometimes your heart gives a silly hop, step and jump; and then it skips a beat or two when a girl looks in a certain way, or a certain strain of music comes from her throat. But when men fight, those things don't count.

"We go back to the beginning," said Easter, unaware of Hurtado's impatience. "How'd you find out that Marigny and Don Ricardo were beasts?"

"Except for me, they wouldn't have dared to steal the Seabold lands."

Her eyes found the face of Seabold and jumped away from him to Easter again.

"But they could base everything on you, eh?" asked Easter. "You could transfer most of your father's rights—his so-called rights—to Marigny, eh? And then Marigny would open his purse to Don Ricardo."

"That's the way it was to be," she agreed.

"Well, if you agreed to it, what happened?"

"They wanted me to sign over the deeds to the Universal Fruit Company this morning. I couldn't do it."

"Why couldn't you do it?" asked Easter.

"I don't know."

"You knew beforehand, though. It was all arranged. You knew what they expected of you. I suppose?"

"Yes," she said.

"Then why wouldn't you do what they wanted? They raised all this hullabaloo thinking that you'd give them the legal basis, and that would cut off all the international complications. Isn't that true?"

She was silent.

"Why couldn't you go through with your part of it?" insisted Easter.

"I don't know. I couldn't."

"Give her a drink of something," said Hurtado. "And then leave her, Jack. The men are waiting."

"Agosto, be patient," said Easter. "I want to see how much she lies, and how much of a spy she is."

"That's silly," said Seabold.

The general turned upon him a terrible eye.

"Be silent!" he commanded.

Seabold started. He was silent.

"You don't lie?" asked Easter.

"No," said the girl.

"A trembling lip and tear in the eye don't make a bit of difference to me," said Easter.

She straightened. She gripped her hands into fists.

"After you refused to work with 'em—you don't give us any reason for not working with them, though?"

"I saw four thousand men stupidly walked into a trap!" cried the girl. "Is that reason enough?"

"Your refusing to work with 'em—that wouldn't keep them from butchering this outfit," said Easter, "though it might make them try to effect a compromise if they could. They tried the compromise, in fact, and it didn't work."

"Ha!" said Hurtado. "Now I see!"

"I told them," said Mary Cosgrave, "that if they could end the thing without fighting I'd sign over every right I had in the world."

"When the compromise didn't work, what did they do?"

"They put me in a hut in the village. They put a guard over me. I escaped."

"Why?"

"I don't know. I had to try to get away from them… The sneaking—the cowards—the beasts. I hate them!"

"Stop crying," said Easter. "Crying doesn't make a bit of difference to us."

She stopped crying.

"How did you manage to escape?" asked Easter.

"The rain came smashing down. I got out a dirty blanket and lay down on one of the beds in the room. It was damp and cold. I tried to sleep. Then a door opened and one of the men looked in at me. I heard him mutter that it was all right, because I was asleep. The door closed. I wondered what was 'all right.' I got up and looked out the rear window. There was no longer any guard there. I pushed the window open and climbed through. Then I started straight down toward the valley. That was all."

"How do you mean that?" demanded Easter. "Why was it all? You had their sentries to pass, and their patrols."

"The sentries were so far apart, I just waited till they had disappeared into the rain. Then I went on. The patrol didn't come near me."

"You were able to come right through?"

"Yes."

Easter turned around on Hurtado.

"Now is it wasted time that I've been putting in?" he asked.

"What do you mean, my general?"

"Tell me, Agosto—is that the strongest part of their lines, lying straight ahead?"

"Of course."

"Where they have most of their big guns around the end of the railroad?"

"That's true also, of course."

"They've stripped themselves so bare that even this girl could get through," said Easter. "Do we march the men on to the hills?"

"Ay, and they have the fewest men! They look on that as their stone wall that we won't attempt. They're pouring men onto the other three sides to bottle us up for use in the morning. But they've stripped themselves so bare that even this girl could get through! What do you say to me, Agosto? Do we march the men straight on to the hills?"

IT WAS NOT the picture that had filled the mind of Seabold. He had thought of generalship as a thing of maps, long forethought, a checkerboard brilliance of tactics: but now he knew that it could be a sudden decision based on the chance report that a girl brought into camp. For some such turn of chance Easter had

been waiting. Perhaps through all his campaigns it had been the same thing—a casual idleness of mind until the opening came through which he could strike.

Easter snapped at him: "Get out your men. Keep 'em bunched. March 'em straight on toward the hills. They've got La Merced in their blood, and they'll have to be our shock troops. Start now!"

As Seabold went out of the tent, he heard Easter saying: "Now tell me what changed your mind this morning. Yesterday you were one of them, so what changed you today?"

"I don't know!" said the girl, and began to cry.

Seabold, hearing the sobbing, stopped on the dim verge of the sound. It made him feel a little sick, a little unclean. After all, she had brought in the news on which Easter was acting. Then a fresh downpouring of the rain drowned out the sound, and he went on to his small regiment.

He drew them into a huddle. He put his arms around two pairs of shoulders and said, loudly: "Lennox has moved most of his men to the other sides of the valley. He's only left a few with the guns up there on the hills straight ahead... You remember the guns at La Merced?"

They yelled like wolves. For his own part, a cold lump was in his throat and his teeth wanted to chatter; the instant good cheer of these fellows amazed him.

He said: "We don't want noise. We don't want yelling. Machetes will be better than rifles. They won't make the noise. Sling your rifles and have your machetes in hand, and follow me. Pass the word."

He heard the word pass out in a ripple; then he was marching ahead of them through the mud.

Marching was not the word. It was a slithering and a sloshing through the slime. Again and again he lost his footing. The men about him pulled him up. He saw that he was holding them and their bare feet back. They could have passed him with the neatest ease, as they had passed him at Merced

More guns were speaking. Always the thin screech of the shell seemed to pass directly overhead, making him shorten his neck and bend his knees; right afterward came the boom of the report. Sometimes he could hear the shell plop into the mud, then the dull explosion. Those men at the three-inch guns had it easy, with tarpaulins up, no doubt, to shield them from the worst of the weather. Down there in the valley it was walking through mud, sometimes knee-deep; and often the blackness seemed to choke up the lungs as though the air were growing muddy, also.

The rain was a thing to hear of but never to believe. The Government forces were doing everything in good army style, using advanced methods and firing star shells and rockets from time to time on all four fronts, but these lights were only dim smothers in the torrents of rain that shaded out everything with a billion pencil strokes.

There was such rain that it got inside his collar, inside his oiled silk, and ran in slimy cold currents down his back and over the vital, tender warmth of his belly.

When he reached the little arroyo which the horses had forded with such ease, the water rose to his breast, then to his chin. He was gasping with the weight of the current, and then the cold of the stream. When he got to the farther shore, he threw away the useless cloak. It was only a small weight but every ounce counted.

While his men came over the arroyo, he lay down in the mud and lifted his boots, one by one, to let the liquid burden of the water run out of them. When he got up again, he reached back and pulled off the clots of mud which adhered to him.

Then he went on.

They were commencing the slope, at about the place where the tent for the conference had been pitched, when a rocket sailed far out from the southern line and dropped with a stream of fire right in the middle of the Hurtadistas. Even so, it gave him only a partial glimpse of the picture behind him of other contingents struggling over the arroyos, and still others stretching back into the mist as far as his struggling eye could reach. The four thousand never had seemed a tithe as numerous as this. They came on now like the flow of a dark river, a solid, endless column.

THE SLOPE of the hill grew sharper. He had to turn his feet sidewise and drive them hard into the loose, slippery mud. Even so he went down every minute or two.

The men about him were having trouble enough to keep their

own feet without bothering to assist their leader. They panted and gasped and whispered their curses.

Sounds came up from the rear and toward his left. He heard the working of many feet under the roar of the rain. Another section of the Hurtadistas was challenging his lead.

He could see the hills in front of him as black and sheer as the wall of a house—or so they seemed to him—when a rifle clanged on the left, a voice screeched, turned into a horrible bubbling sound, and was still.

A moment later half a dozen men were yelling from the slope: *"Quien viva? Quien viva?"*

The answer bellowed through the noise of the rain in the familiar voice of James Princeton Easter, crying, "Hurtado! *Viva* Hurtado! Up and at them, boys!... San Esteban... Hurtado!"

The whole mass of soldiers that swarmed behind Seabold took up that cry like madmen. Up a slope where he could barely stagger, they fairly ran. If they could not run erect, they ran on their hands and knees.

That black hillside broke out into a flame of rockets and flares that even the weight of the rain could not dim. It was bright as fire, but through that fire the soldiers were running at the crest of the hill; and down the slope, far down into the valley, other thousands of the Hurtadistas were yelling, a river of sound. Then, left and right, rapid fire began to blaze from the three-inch guns. He could realize that they were being shot at far too great an angle, as though they had been given range for the lower valley, and the gunners had not time to depress the muzzles of the cannon.

His own throat was aching as it had ached at La Merced because he was yelling with every step he took, yelling and stumbling in the mud and staggering up again, until his automatic was the centre of a great clotted mass of mud.

He saw his men leaping against the light of the flares, and against the snake tongues of gunfire. Yes, it was like a fire. Some

"Mary, I love you!"

"Are you a great liar?" she asked.

of the men shrivelled up on the verge of it; others leaped into the flames, as it were.

Then he was up there at the sketchy little line of shallow trenches, and the world fell into place again. The slope of the hill was not a sheer ascent of black tar, but a rounding grade. The blazing line of battle degenerated into occasional rockets. And everywhere before him the resistance had died out... He could hear the yells of *Viva* Hurtado ringing as far as the village houses, as far as the many sidetracks where the corps of flat- and box-cars were assembled by the industry of Don Ricardo and the money of Marigny. These objects were obscurely viewed not by the lights which they carried but by the flashes and the flares from the farther trenches, right and left, where fighting still went on.

He stumbled across the trenches—mere rifle pits half flooded with water. He washed the mud from his hands, from his automatic, in that water, and clambered up the farther side. There he tried the gun and it exploded.

That was the first shot he had fired during two battles!

A shadow detached itself from the soil and wriggled toward him, moaning: "Water! Water! In the name of sweet Jesus, water, señor!"

That voice from the ground mired him down more than mud. He had to do something. There was a battle going on, and he was out of it. He wished that the roar of the rain and the noise of the firing would cover up that voice which moaned on the ground. He was a general, and he ought to be leading, instead of drawing out his canteen and holding the shaggy head of a single wounded man.

"What are you, brother?" he asked, as the frantic hand of the wounded soldier grasped the canteen.

He could hear the water gurgling down the fellow's throat. Then the gasping voice: "Jesus and the Virgin reward you! I am Manuel Pampillo. But my heart is with Hurtado. *Viva...*"

He began to cough up bubbles of blood. Seabold saw that clutching gesture of both hands to the breast and ran on toward the noise of the fighting. There had been a crazy ecstasy back there at La Merced; there had been a moment of battle madness when he was clambering up the impossible, greasy face of the hill; but now he felt like a lonely, frightened little boy in the rain.

Somewhere voices were crying: "La Merced! La Merced!"

HE MADE for that familiar cheer. It came from a place where a whole battery of the rapid-fire guns was being turned to serve against the crest of the hills as they swept back in a dim and disappearing curve through the night. On the left, the valley seemed a sea. The rain could not be seen to sink into the shadow of it. Behind him, he could make out the dim hordes of the Hurtadistas still pouring up like figures out of the ocean. Men were shouting: "Victory! *Viva* Hurtado!" The three-inch guns began to batter away at the blackness.

He was in a swirl of the men of La Merced. Someone was shouting in a terrible voice to commence firing, to open up with rifles. That was Easter. How had his older legs taken him up the slope and to the point of contact as quickly as this? And then he made out blackness moving in blackness as a mass of men poured toward them over the crest of the hills.

He shouted a repetition of the order. All about him he could hear the voices yelling: "The little general! He is with us! Give them hell, *amigos!*"

They were lying flat. Occasional flares showed them to him as living clots of mud, but calmly pulling bullets out of their belts and shooting at the shadows through the rain.

Those fellows came on yelling: "The Republic! The Republic! *Viva* Don Ricardo!"

Their front disappeared down a small swale in the ground. The mass of them followed, so that the hill was crawling with life. The three-inch guns kept roaring. The rifles chattered a higher pitched nonsense. The front of the charge did not appear again.

He himself, standing erect, fired until his automatic was empty.

"For our sake, my general, don't let them kill you and our luck!"

He had to keep saying to himself: "It's a battle. It isn't a crazy dream. It's a battle—in San Esteban!"

He reloaded his gun and struck the detaining hands away as he stood up. A general has to stand up. He has to be seen.

The forefront of the Ricardistas did not appear again. The shallow swale of ground swallowed them completely, like a hollow chasm. Now he could see them spilling away to the right and to the left. All the Hurtadistas were shouting, "Victory!" They jumped up and began to dance. They splattered mud like dogs shaking themselves after rolling in a ditch. Some of the filth flew into the face of Seabold. He spat.

The huge, hoarse voice of Easter was calling: "Seabold! Seabold! Where are you, Joe?"

He floundered through the mud and found the general.

"Here, general!" he called.

"Was it beautiful, Joe?" asked the general. "A little child shall lead us—a little girl *did* lead us, didn't she? Keep these guns going while I begin to load our ragamuffins on the trains for San Esteban. Just fire now and then... Good old Hurtado is holding them on the other flank... Good-bye, Joe!"

And he was gone, shouting out of the darkness, gathering men about him. And Seabold was left alone in that horrible confusion of mud and men and guns.

THE THING was clear enough in his mind, finally. The picture was simple enough. Don Ricardo and even that clever dark devil of a Marigny had made their mistake in stripping too many men from their strongest point in order to close the lines around the rest of their four-walled trap. No doubt they had their pictures of a wretched army of rebels submitting to the rain and the mud down there in the heart of the valley, or at the most merely preparing to break out where the hills were lowest or, most probably, toward the rear and the jungle, where there were no hills at all. Now, with darkness and the mud to flounder through, the army of Don Ricardo could come up only slowly to the point where the rebels had broken through. Some of them would have long miles of trudging.

This was war. Blindman's Buff, guesswork, luck.

Still he saw no good way out of the trouble. For when the morning came, Don Ricardo would be in possession of forces still nearly fourfold those of the revolution, and how could even a lucky General Easter stand against them?

There were no more massed attacks on the battery which he commanded. From the other side of the breach which they had driven through Marigny's lines, however, ten minutes of uproar broke out a little later. It died away. The cheering for Hurtado told who had won. And they were safe, probably, until the morning light came.

But the morning did not find them in that place. Back where the cars were ranged along the sidings, the army of the revolution was drawn gradually and loaded onto the trains. The absurd little engines began to snort and labor to get the long trains in motion.

Hurtado went off with the first consignment to make an entry into San Esteban City as soon as possible. Seventy-five miles, at fifteen miles an hour—he would get in about the breaking of the day.

Easter and Seabold went with the last division, in the midst of a great turmoil. All the heavy guns were left in place, the breech blocks taken out of the cannon, thus rendering them useless. Only ammunition was taken in quantities till the big dumps were cleaned out. Then as the last train pulled slowly away, a final swarm of the soldiers tore up the tracks behind it with charges of dynamite. Even if Don Ricardo could conjure cars and engines out of the air, he would have no track on which to use them.

THE REARMOST car of the train was an excellent caboose after the fashion of American cars of the same sort. In this sat General James Princeton Easter with certain cheerful trifles which he had been able to pick up at the looted headquarters of Don Ricardo and Tom Lennox. He had rum and wine and lemons, and all that he needed for good cheer. He had a bucket of water, too, in which he had bathed off the mud after removing the majority of his clothes, so that he sat now in damp underwear and a monocle, helping himself to rum punch and serving Joseph Seabold with the same. On the other side of the car, bedded down on a heap of blankets, slept Mary Cosgrave, exhausted so that her lips were blue, and a blue shadow underlined her eyes also. Seabold sat with his back to her.

He merely hooked a thumb over his shoulder and asked: "How?"

The general made a pause.

"You can be a mean young blighter," he said. "So could the Admiral, for that matter. Can't you be sorry for a poor girl who tried to do the right thing at the last minute?"

"Yes, yes, I know about that," said Seabold carelessly. "But how did she happen to get here?"

"I couldn't leave her alone, could I, in that mob of men? I

appointed a squad of four to see that she got up the hill right behind me, and that's the way she came. She used her own feet part of the way and they carried her the rest... Pretty thing, Joe, isn't she?"

He leaned to stare into the shadow cast by Seabold's chair.

"Pretty?" said Seabold. He looked into space. "I suppose so," he said. "Pour me another whack of that punch, will you, general?"

The general observed: "The young generation has gone to hell, Joe." He poured the tin cup full of punch. "No romance left in the world. No two hearts that beat as one, and all that. I'm glad I'm getting old."

"You can't get old," said Seabold. "Here you are riding off as secure as can be—and yet there'll be fifteen thousand men on the way to San Esteban City tomorrow, and plenty of guns along with them to blast the town down around our ears."

The general stared.

"Guns? You mean the three-inchers?"

"Of course that's what I mean."

"Joe," said the general, "do you know how far it is from here to San Esteban City?"

"Seventy miles?"

"Of mud!" said the general.

He allowed this information to sink in for a time, then he added: "In addition to all that, we've gutted their food supplies and their quartermaster stores. What we couldn't carry away, we burned. Look back there." He pointed to the dying smudge of fire far away in the rain.

"Seventy-five miles. That's not far. It's not even as bad as the jungle," said Seabold.

"Our boys cut through because they had to win or die," said the general. "These poor blighters only have to desert. When the morning comes they find us gone, themselves licked, and nothing but deep, soft mud between them and San Esteban City. Will they stay together? Will they die for Don Ricardo? Not even if he had money. And he hasn't any money. It's all locked up in his bank back there in San Esteban City. In his bank and in his palace. And we, my lad, are going to help ourselves!"

They tore up three miles of track with blasting. Then Moreno, insatiable of work with his new title around his neck, took command of a rearguard detail which was to blast away twenty miles more and remain on guard at the end of the track that was left, to watch the movements of the enemy. With double rations of *agua dolce* and treble pay, that rearguard was rewarded for failing to join in the triumphal entry into San Esteban.

"You mean," said Seabold, after long thought, "that the war's over?"

"Over and done with, and so's Marigny—in this part of the world," said Easter. "And so's Don Ricardo. Marigny's goods are proclaimed forfeit to the Republic, for engendering rebellion and what not. What are Marigny's goods? Oh, just about a million in hard cash. That's all. Universal Fruit won't be so proud of its president when it hears the news of the battle of Cristobal; not when it learns how the good honest dollars are jingling in the pockets of Hurtado, Easter and Joseph Seabold. And what is your company going to think of you, you young runagate? Is it going to change its presidential mind? If you don't get some wires from Kelvin licking the Seabold boots all clean of mud, call me a baby and a half-wit. But it's time to think, *amigo*. It's time to plan and deliberate. San Esteban is ours. How are we going to use it?"

SEABOLD USED it for sleep.

He was blind with fatigue that never had been cleansed from his mind since that terrible march through the jungle with Jack Easter. He was so sick with weariness that he retained only a dreamy memory of the march through the streets of San Esteban City in what had fallen, luckily, to a mere light drizzle of rain.

A march it had to be, and not a ride in trucks and automobiles. Hurtado had got hold of a batch of old flags, in some way. He had the first division of that muddy army behind his horse. General Easter headed the second batch. And behind Seabold came the men with the blue cotton rags tied around their arms. Every householder and shopkeeper along the way turned out to raise a hearty cheer, though the news had come on San Esteban City so freshly that some men were still writing in chalk on their walls, "*Viva* Hurtado!" when they had to turn and cheer the living presence of the old revolutionary.

Crackers were set off, guns fired, cannon boomed a salute when they reached the presidential mansion. More cannon were firing hastily from the House of Deputies.

Most of the deputies, it was rumored, had fled from the town.

But when Seabold reached the presidential mansion, he wanted only one thing, and that was a bed. He got an entire suite of gaudy chambers. None of it existed for him except the bed under its white memorial draping of mosquito netting. He dived through that white mist and was instantly asleep.

Afterward, a persistent voice roused him.

A *mozo*, half frightened and half grinning, said: "La Merced, señor! La Merced! The men of La Merced are serenading señor, the little general. They wait for you outside. This way! This way to the balcony. If you will put on these clothes…"

He pointed out a whole array of gold-braided finery laid out on a couch, with gleaming boots and a sword beside it. But the fine display made no impression on the drugged brain of Seabold. All in those jungle rags, dirty as an alley cat, he stumbled out onto the balcony, to find the dazzle of a clear sun and a vast blue sky overhead, and beneath him a wild uproar from hundreds of men who wore blue bands around their left arms. They were his men of La Merced, now dressed in their best, and every breast decorated with at least one shining medal!

They began to laugh and point out his rags.

"The little general!" they shouted. For he would always be a delightful jest to them, it seemed.

They hushed one another to a silence. Seabold folded his soiled arms on the stone railing of the balcony and said: "I wondered what I had with me at La Merced. Now I know it was five hundred cats. Because you can do without sleep, but I cannot. God bless you. *Adios!*"

It was the shortest speech ever made in San Esteban, and it was the most applauded. He went back to his bed and lay there in torpor or sleep for another day, only rousing now and then to eat, and then falling asleep again.

When he roused, it was in a different world. For the House of Deputies had reassembled, called back by Hurtado's proclamations of amnesty. It had reassembled all the more willingly because word had come in of the swift dissolution of the army of Don Ricardo in the mud, and the disappearance of the late President and Marigny.

There followed for the deputies a glorious all-night session, in which first of all they wiped out all the acts of Don Ricardo's regime. In the second place they passed a series of new laws, laws which were designed by honest Hurtado to make San Esteban forever glorious and honest and free. After that, they passed a few other laws. To Generals Easter and Seabold were given the noble titles "Friends of the Republic!" and certain special medals and honors; among others the right of picking flowers in the plaza of the city! They went farther. They gave to Señor the General Seabold by permanent concession, never to be taken from his company, all the lands which the Admiral ever had held by a less lasting right. They granted him certain moneys also, to repair losses and damages incurred during the late unhappy war.

THAT WAS why Seabold, when he finally wakened in earnest,

found stacks of telegrams beside his bed. One from Kelvin was very interesting. The Seabold Company, it appeared, had changed its mind. It realized the magnificent courage, the wonderful forethought, the extreme genius which Seabold had shown since his arrival in San Esteban. In consequence, Kelvin had resigned from his office, and Joseph Seabold was unanimously elected president in his place.

"Bananas!" said Joseph Seabold, and allowed the telegram to fall to the floor.

He took a cold bath, shaved the dense hair from his face, washed the last mud out of his hair, and sat down to breakfast in a shaft of bright golden sunlight; his own house, it appeared, was now being refurnished and made worthy of his presence at the expense of the Republic itself.

While he ate, he read, with occasional halts in his munchings, occasional popping of the eyes, all the news up to date in the San Esteban morning paper. It was chiefly featured by pictures of the glorious new president, Hurtado, surrounded by a border of flags. But there was also a picture of a rather scrawny youth who leaned in rags on one of the presidential balconies. Beneath it was a glowing account of "the little general."

Señor Seabold hastily poured some rum into his coffee and drank it down.

Then Easter came in. He shone like a statue in whites.

"The younger generation can't take it, Joe," he said by way of greeting. "I've been drunk twice and sober again, since we reached San Esteban City. And look at you and your wasted time."

"General, you have a new string for your monocle, I see," said Seabold.

"Before I retire to my estates in the mountains," said the general, "I thought I'd drop in on you."

"Are they going to damn me with that nickname the rest of my life? Are they going to laugh at me forever?" mourned Seabold.

"They'll laugh at you and love you," said the general. "Hurtado wants to see you."

"Good old Hurtado," said Seabold. "Is he happy?"

"Happy as a surgeon," said the general, "binding up some of the wounds of his people and planning to knife them all over again—for their own good... A lot of foreign and native reporters want to see you, too."

"To the devil with them," said Seabold.

"You can't say that," answered James Princeton Easter. "Give me a dash of that rum—you can't say that. Joe. You're a public man from now to the end of your days... But there's one thing on your conscience, Joe. You haven't forgotten, have you, the rotten thing that you did?"

"What?" asked Seabold.

The general shook his head gloomily.

"I thought you were a clean-bred one," he said. "But don't tell me that there's really a yellow streak."

"I've been half dead with sleep, general," said Seabold, startled. "I may have been waked suddenly; I may have said or done something. For lord's sake, what is it?"

"You'll have to come with me and face it," said the general.

"But what is it?"

"Don't bother me with questions. You'll realize when you come face to face with it, Seabold. Every man has something in his past, and there's never a free moment for those that don't face it."

He led the way from the room, while Seabold wretchedly followed him. The good rum in the coffee, that should have heartened him, merely set his pulse trembling.

THEY WENT far down the corridor. They passed, indeed, to the other end of the presidential mansion, where the rooms overlooked the gardens. There the general opened a door and showed Seabold into a room done in blue and white and mirrors. A delicate fragrance filled the air here, perhaps blown in through the windows that showed him the full riot of the gardens outside. And yet there was a suspicious difference.

"Mary!" shouted the general, in his Stentor's battle voice.

Seabold, startled, turned only in time to see the door closing on the grinning face of James Easter. He grasped the knob of the door; but a key grated in the turning lock.

"Coming, general!" called the voice of Mary Cosgrave.

He saw her, first, in a long mirror, all in the coolest white, an image wavering toward him like something rising through water. Then she was under the entrance arch.

When she saw him, she stopped. A frightened deer—he thought of something like that and threw the silly image away. It was one of those beginnings in life; it was one of those things that never will go out of the mind; he knew that the instant was eternal for him, as he stared at her.

Somewhere in the background of his mind, he could remember having stared at her and come to certain conclusions. That was a million years ago, before he had been able to sleep and cleanse his mind of all its darkness and folly.

She paused only for a moment, growing redder and redder. Afterward, she came straight up to him.

"I know what's happened," she said. "The general told you everything."

"No," said Seabold.

"It was cruel of him," said the girl. "He didn't understand… You look white and sick, Joseph. Will you come over here and sit down by the window?"

He went over and sat down by the window. There was a bird singing its feathers on end at the top of a flowering bush in the garden. It was like a divinely inspired messenger; it sang straight to the trembling heart of Seabold.

She sat opposite him, very erect.

"I know he told you," said the girl.

"He didn't," said Seabold.

"Didn't he? He didn't tell you just *why* I went down into the valley that night?"

Such relief began to shine in her eyes that Seabold leaned forward to look at her more carefully.

"He didn't tell me. He just left me here, like a yokel," he said. He added, without the slightest appropriateness: "You're as beautiful..." He pointed out the window. She would have to understand what he meant.

"Joseph," she said, "I don't want you to say your set speech, please."

He began to feel himself cornered. Then he saw a slight tremor in her throat. A pulse was beating in there, a shadowy linger of blue was tapping at a racing speed. He tried to count it. His brain grew very dizzy.

"He told me only one thing that counted," said Seabold. "It was about a fight—about a battle—when in doubt..."

He stood up. She rose with him.

"Joseph," she cried out, "you look terribly white!"

"Why shouldn't I?" said he. "Why shouldn't I when my heart's going smash?... Mary, I love you!"

"Are you a great liar?" she asked. "Are you saying a piece the dear silly old general taught you?"

"I love you!" said Seabold, the tremor passing out of his heart into his voice.

"Well?" said the girl, smiling.

And suddenly he saw that she was waiting.